PENTHESILEA

RISE OF AN AMAZON

A NOVEL

STEPHANIE VANISE

Cover design by Stephanie Neroes
 Edited by Beatrice Kimber

Library of Congress Cataloging-in-Publication Data
Names: Neroes, Stephanie Vanise, author
Title: Penthesilea: Rise of an Amazon
Description: First Edition | Stephanie Neroes

Identifiers: ISBN: 979-8-89860-154-6 paperback | 979-8-89965-916-4 ebook

Published in the United States of America by Stephanie Neroes

For my mother — an Amazon in her own right.

The one who said,
"You should write a movie about Penthesilea,"
believing I could — before I ever did.

And for every woman who has ever had to fight,
to protect, to endure, or to find herself —

You are the story.

PROLOGUE

Darkness…

Long ago, during the Age of Heroes…
There was a young woman named Otrera.
She was my mother.

—

Twilight bleeds across the sky, bruising it with streaks of fading gold and deepening violet. Beyond the crumbling city walls, dust coils in soft, snaking plumes around the legs of a lone figure, her shadow stretching long against the fading light.

Otrera — seventeen. Gaunt, sun-browned, and worn thin by hardship. She moves with slow, deliberate steps, hauling a water vessel nearly as heavy as she is. The jar sloshes with each stride, its clay surface slick with sweat and grit. Her hands, wrapped in dirty cloth, clutch it tightly.

Sweat beads along her temples. Her gaze is fixed on the stone walls ahead — cold, silent, indifferent.

When my sisters and I were children, she would whisper
the truth of our nation into the dark — a story known by
few and understood by fewer.

The house is a dim, sunless shell. The air smells of old clay, sour wine, and the stagnant heat of a place long deprived of joy.

Otrera enters.

A man lounges in the corner. Her husband. Thick-bodied and slack-jawed, his tunic stained with wine, his gaze, dull and bitter, fixes on her.

He doesn't rise. Just scowls from where he lies sprawled in the gloom.

"Otrera. My stomach rages like a beast."

She exhales quietly. Her chin dips. Eyes lowered — not out of respect, but control.

She had been given to him, A man unworthy of her silence.

He stumbles upright, wine mug in hand, movements unsteady. He sways toward her like a crumbling tower.

"Feed me this—"

His knees give way.

He crashes to the ground with a grunt. The mug thuds beside him, wine spilling into the dirt. Otrera watches, unmoving.

She lifts her foot, nudges his side.

No response.

Then she draws her leg back and drives a sharp, deliberate kick into his ribs.

He groans — then begins to snore.

She stares at his bloated form. The fire in her eyes is not fear.

The forest hums with quiet night sounds — crickets, rustling leaves, a whisper of wind through cypress trees.

Nature's melody morphs into labored breathing and a pounding heartbeat.

Otrera stands in a moonlit clearing. Her body has changed—sinewy now, marked with sweat, callus and grit. Her tunic clings to her, soaked with effort. Her hands are torn and bleeding through their bandages.

She swings a club.

Each strike echoes through the trees. The air splits. Wood shudders. Again. And again.

Muscles ripple. Pain rises. Still, she strikes — steady, ruthless. Each blow more precise than the last.

Her breathing deepens. Her eyes narrow in focus.

She lifts the club once more and delivers one final, bone-jarring blow. The wood cracks beneath the force.

She trained relentlessly... honing her battle skills, preparing for the moment that would result in her freedom.

The house again.

Otrera enters with a small loaf of bread clutched in

her hand. Her steps are measured. She doesn't speak. Before she can place the bread down, a hand smashes across her face.

Her head snaps to the side.

Her husband leers, slurring with laughter and drink.

Her fingers twitch. She straightens. And swings.

Her fist drives into his face with a sickening crack. He staggers back.

They struggle. A blur of limbs and rage.

She is smaller, but stronger now. Sharper.

She grabs the club from beneath the sleeping mat.

She raises it.

And brings it down.

The wood strikes his skull with a heavy, splitting sound.

His body drops. Blood pools from beneath his head, thick and slow.

She stares at him—expressionless.

The club slips from her hand.

She walks out the door.

Inspired...

The city sleeps beneath a moonwashed sky. The stone streets gleam faintly with dew.

Then—a sharp whistle cuts the silence.

Groans follow. Grunts. Screams.

The soft, wet thuds of bodies hitting the ground.

Women flood the streets—barefoot, breathless, bloodied.

Daughters wielding kitchen blades.

Mothers brandishing farming sickles.

Sisters with nothing but fists.

Their faces are grim. Their eyes blaze — wide, wild, and unflinching.

The fearless and unbroken women rose. And every man within the walls... fell.

Cries pierce the chaos.

Young boys cry out for mothers vanishing into the dark.

Small hands reach for shadows.

One boy stumbles through the street. His name unknown, but history will carve it in stone: Bellerophon.

Tears streak the dirt on his cheeks.

Beneath his right eye, a fresh scar cuts clean and red across the skin.

They seized what they never thought to be possible…

Otrera rides through the city on horseback, silhouetted against flickering firelight.

Her expression is unreadable as she surveys the devastation.

Her eyes meet the boy's—just for a moment.

A flicker passes between them.

Recognition? Defiance?

Something deeper?

Then she spurs the horse forward.

And rides on — leading her sisters beyond the burning city.

Freedom. But not without great cost.

The forest is thick with night.

Greek soldiers ride hard, their hooves pounding the earth. The light from their torches dances across leaves and bark. Armor creaks. Eyes scan the dark.

They slow.

A tracker dismounts and kneels beside a scuffed patch of earth, brushing it with his fingers.

When word of their uprising spread…

A faint snap echoes nearby. A twig.

The soldiers freeze.

A shadow moves.

An arrow whistles through the air and sinks into the tracker's chest. He gasps—and crumples.

From the darkness, they come.

Otrera and her warriors surge forward—blades drawn, arrows loosed, fists hammering. They descend like a storm, swift and silent, driven not by vengeance, but by necessity.

Later, another skirmish. Another blood-washed night beneath the trees.

The enemy is larger, stronger. But slower.

Otrera steps forward to face the biggest among them—a soldier broad as a bull, veins thick along his arms.

He raises his fists and roars.

They jeered... how dare women fight against men?

She doesn't flinch. She ducks, pivots, and drives her blade across his throat. The skin parts clean. Blood sprays.

He drops, twitching.

She steps over his corpse and wipes her blade, breath calm.

They killed only to survive.

CHAPTER 1

Themyscira — Summer, 1224 BCE

Sunlight pours in golden sheets across a pristine coastline.

The sea breathes against the sand, brushing it with white lace. The air smells of salt and warmth — the kind that wraps itself around your skin like silk.

Across the Aegean, where the River Thermodon coils like a silver serpent, they found it — a land forgotten by the world, untouched by war and becomes their sanctuary—Themyscira.

Otrera walks the length of the beach. Her steps are steady, barefoot in the foam, the waves lapping gently at her ankles. Her skin is bronze and sun-kissed. Her eyes are closed, tilted toward the sea breeze.

Each breath fills her chest with peace.

But peace is never without memory.

The sky groans.

A white blaze splits the heavens — sudden, blinding, fierce. It falls toward the earth like a sword drawn by the gods.

It strikes the beach with thunder.

A shock-wave ripples through sand and bone. Birds scatter. The sea reels. Light bursts from the impact, and when it fades — a figure stands where the fire landed.

He does not belong to this world.

Tall. Solid. Shadowed in divine brilliance.

Ares.

God of War.

He walks forward, barefoot, sand parting beneath him. His form shifts — not monstrous, but noble, human in shape. Rough-hewn like a warrior who has tasted blood and fire. Scarred hands. Eyes the color of burnt gold.

He raises a hand — not in dominance, but devotion.

"You are the one," he says.

His fingers brush her cheek. Not cruel. Not kind. Reverent, like touching sacred stone.

"Such beauty," he says."Such fury"

He lowers his hand.

"Be my bride," he offers. "Bear my children?"

Themyscira — Fall, 1219 BCE

The shadows of dusk press softly against the stone walls of Otrera's private chamber. The warm orange light filters through slatted shutters, catching on the hanging bronze charms and woven tapestries that sway gently in the ocean breeze. And then—

A scream slices the stillness.

Otrera jolts upright, her voice raw with pain, echoing off the high ceilings. Her back arches instinctively, hands gripping the furs beneath her as a new wave of agony rolls through her body. The sacred pain — the pain of birth.

Her legs are lifted, thighs trembling, sweat clinging

to her brow like a second skin. A seasoned Amazon midwife kneels between her, calm and focused, hands steady as marble. She murmurs words that do not need to be heard — her confidence flows like a river. This is not her first birth, nor her last.

Beside the laboring queen stand two small sentinels: Hippolyta, three years old, her eyes wide with curiosity and unease; and Antiope, only a year younger, silent, clutching her sister's hand. They do not speak. They only watch.

A final cry tears from Otrera's throat as her body convulses with one last push.

The newborn slides into the world, glistening and wailing, and the midwife moves with practiced grace, wrapping the child swiftly in soft cloth, swaddling the girl before placing her into Otrera's waiting arms.

A breath escapes the queen — not just of relief, but of reverence. The storm within her quiets. Her eyes soften as they fall upon the blood-slicked face of the infant.

"You will be named Penthesilea..." Otrera whispers, voice thick with exhaustion and awe. "Breaker of hearts and bringer of sorrow."

She turns to her daughters, beckoning them closer.

"Hippolyta. Antiope. Meet your sister."

The girls step hesitantly forward. Tiny fingers reach for the wrappings, brushing gently across the infant's chest. The baby coos — a small, curious sound, the very first breath of a future warrior.

A lull hums softly in the air — Otrera's voice, low

and warm, soothing the child in her arms. It's not a song of
joy, nor grief, but something in between — a melody
ancient as the stones beneath their feet.

From the edges of the chamber, shadows stir. A
group of Amazon warriors enters with reverent quiet, their
faces lit by firelight and wonder. They move without
words, forming a loose circle around their queen. Their
eyes fall upon the infant with unspoken reverence. There is
no need to announce the birth of a daughter here. The air
itself seems to hold its breath in tribute.

*Mother's courage not only gave birth to a nation of
women…*

Themyscira — Summer, 1207 BCE

The sun stands low in the sky, casting molten
shadows across the shore of Themyscira. The sea is a
mirror of fire and gold, its breath rolling over sand carved
smooth by centuries.

A dozen warriors thunder across the beach. Their
feet strike the earth in unison — not clumsy, but
choreographed. Hair braided, muscles taut, eyes burning
with the joy of exertion. They run not for escape, but for
mastery.

At the front of the charge, Otrera leads. Age has not
dulled her — it has only sharpened her spirit. She ducks
beneath a swinging log suspended by ropes, her body
flowing like water under threat. Behind her, one Amazon
mistimes the dodge — wood grazes her shoulder, tearing

skin. She snarls at the pain, blood slick on her flesh, and drives forward harder, refusing to be slowed.

But a sisterhood of warriors.

Dozens more join the run — mothers, daughters, warriors in their prime and elders still unwilling to yield to time. They laugh, they roar, they jostle like lionesses at the kill. Every movement is a celebration of strength.

Behind a jagged boulder, a girl crouches. Bare feet buried in sand. Breath held. Eyes narrowed. She is still, but not timid — her stillness vibrates with anticipation. She is twelve. Small for her age. But her gaze could strike flint—Penthesilea.

To win was not enough. We needed to endure.

She bursts from cover, legs pumping, body lurching forward in raw pursuit of the tribe that leaves her behind. Her feet sink slightly with every stride, the sand greedy for her motion. She fights it, presses harder, ignoring the ache in her calves, the sweat at her temples.

Then—

A stone. Half-buried. Hidden by the shifting terrain.

She hits it hard. Her ankle buckles. Her body somersaults through the air before crashing into the sand with a jarring thud.

Laughter erupts.

Above her, silhouetted by the sun, stand two girls — statuesque, commanding, older by only a handful of years but elevated like queens on a ridge.

Hippolyta, now fifteen, her face gleaming with sweat and triumph. Antiope, now fourteen, with the cruel smirk of a victor too used to dominance.

"Far too pretty to be a warrior," Hippolyta teases, tilting her head, golden braids catching the breeze.

Antiope's eyes glint with sharpness. "Gathering flowers with Melanippe and Thyra would suit you more."

She pauses.

"Speaking of Hades…"

From the slope behind them, two girls approach — Melanippe, the youngest of the four sisters, and Thyra, both eleven, arms full of fragrant herbs and bright blossoms. They move quickly to Penthesilea, kneeling beside her, brushing sand from her arms and hair.

Hippolyta snorts. "Look at you… Tiny as a beetle."

Penthesilea's jaw clenches. Tears well in her eyes but do not fall.

"Stop mocking me," she says, voice cracking like a reed in wind.

Antiope shrugs. "You run like a goat with broken legs."

Melanippe's eyes flare with anger, but the older sisters have already turned, their laughter trailing behind them like smoke.

Thyra kneels close. "Why do they scorn you so?"

Melanippe's voice is firmer. "Envy floods their

hearts."

Penthesilea watches the retreating silhouettes. "Perhaps they speak truth."

"No," Thyra says gently, fingers on her friend's shoulder. "Their blood runs through you also."

A new voice cuts through the moment. Calm. Commanding. Maternal.

"Thyra is right."

Otrera steps toward them, her figure regal even in casual movement. The sunlight bends around her as if Themyscira itself honors her presence.

She extends a hand.

"Come."

The sky has softened into a sapphire canvas, brushed with the first hints of night. The cliffs rise like ancient sentinels along Themyscira's edge, their shadows long and solemn. A pale moon hangs low, veiled in silver haze. Crickets weave their quiet symphony among the roots of the olive trees, while the breeze hums low through their branches — a gentle voice moving through leaves like whispered memory.

The Garden of Thermodon, sacred and quiet, stretches outward in terraces of stone and brush. Wildflowers bloom in delicate rebellion along the edges of broken columns. Here, amidst boulders littered with scraps of bronze, splinters of wood, and strips of leather, mother and daughter sit — their silhouettes outlined by moonlight and the last vestiges of golden dusk.

Otrera's hands are weathered by time and warfare,

yet when she reaches for Penthesilea's, her touch is tender. The firelight flickering from a nearby brazier catches in her eyes — eyes that have seen kingdoms rise and fall, but never tire of looking into her daughter's face.

"It is time," she says, her voice low, grounded. "You must know how you came to be."

Penthesilea sits perfectly still, the weight of her mother's gaze anchoring her. There is no fear in her eyes — only questions unspoken. Otrera studies her closely. The sharpness of her jawline, the storm held just behind her gaze, the way she holds herself — upright, unyielding — as if the world were already pressing against her and she welcomed the pressure.

"So much of your father burns in you."

Penthesilea does not respond, though her breath catches.

She never spoke of him, her thoughts stir, *or men at all. Their stories are forbidden.*

Otrera turns her face slightly, eyes catching a sliver of moonlight.

"Shortly after we settled here, he came to me…" she pauses, watching her daughter carefully. "From above."

Penthesilea blinks. "From the stars?"

"From Mount Olympus."

Silence passes between them like the wind.

"He watched," Otrera continues, "as I freed myself

and my sisters. He descended not as a conqueror, but in awe. To ask me to be his bride."

Penthesilea's eyes widen, her voice barely above a breath. "Mount Olympus? Is that not the home of the…"

"Yes, the gods." Otrera answers. "Your father is Ares."

She says it without fear. Without reverence. As if naming a storm that once passed through her life and never left.

"Soon after, Hippolyta and Antiope were born. But before you came…" She hesitates, then softens. "I prayed. I asked for a daughter who would grow to be a great warrior in this world. One made of both our strengths."

Her hands encircle Penthesilea's like a seal being formed.

"Ares heard my prayer and you were born. Small and fiery, like a lion cub." A smile flickers across her lips — brief, but real. "You were a delight. But your birth was no accident. With his blood as your own, you are destined for greatness. Your skills — unparalleled."

She taps her daughter's nose, playful, motherly. A moment of simplicity in a life shaped by war.

"So… you see. Thyra is right. The greatness is within. How brightly it shines… Now that is up to you."

Penthesilea grins, wide and proud, her chest rising with a breath that feels fuller than before. "Why have you not spoke of him before?"

Otrera exhales, not tired — but heavy with knowing. "Being the descendant of a god comes with much weight… responsibility. I wanted to protect you. Allow you to be a true child. So… when the time came, your heart was pure."

She pauses. The wind shifts, brushing strands of dark hair across her face.

"But you still have much to learn. War is not a game. It should be waged only when survival demands it." Another pause. This one colder. Deeper.

"Remember that."

Penthesilea nods, solemn now, the weight of her mother's words like iron in her chest.

"Where is Mount Olympus?" she asks.

Otrera tilts her chin upward and lifts a hand toward the sky.

"There. Do you see it? The star that gleams the strongest?"

Penthesilea follows the line of her mother's finger. A single star pierces the blue-black expanse — bright, unmoving, defiant.

She nods.

"That is Sirius. The Dog Star. Mount Olympus lies just beyond it."

Penthesilea smiles quietly. "Sirius," she echoes under her breath, as though the name itself holds power.

"If ever you are lost," Otrera says, her voice now soft as the breeze stirring the trees, "you may look to it. It will lead you home."

They sit in silence for a time. The bronze scraps and twisted bits of armor strewn around them catch the starlight, glinting like forgotten treasure.

"Now," Otrera says, rising to her feet and brushing her hands, "let us see what treasure we can make of this refuse."

They bend to the task, shifting through discarded fragments. The clang of metal on stone rings soft and rhythmic, like the forge of some forgotten god.

From the shadows above, a shape descends in silence — a vulture. It lands atop a nearby rock, its wings folding in slow, eerie motion. Its head tilts as it watches them, dark eyes unblinking.

Otrera's gaze lifts toward it. Her posture stiffens — not fear, but alertness. Something in her muscles tenses, as though recognizing an omen, or remembering a threat long buried.

Though Mother avoided war where she could...

The vulture hisses — not loud, but sinister, guttural, ancient. A sound that does not belong in a place so sacred.

Many craved her fall.

Two years later...

The morning sun kisses the marble bones of Troy, painting the city in shades of gold. Vines twist around towering columns like living jewelry, their leaves glistening with dew. Carved lilies seem to bloom eternally in the stone, untouched by time. The city, at this hour, is quiet — the hush of a storm not yet broken.

But even in the stillness, tension hums like a plucked string.

The world knew the might of her kin…

Inside the palace, behind columns heavy with history and ambition, voices rise not in worship — but in fury.

The bedchamber of Paris, Prince of Troy, is still draped in silks — soft, perfumed, obscenely luxurious. A contrast to the air inside, which crackles with rage.

King Priam stands like stone — unyielding, eyes blazing beneath his bronze circlet. His shoulders square with the weight of a city's survival.

At his side, Hector looms, younger in years but already carved in the image of a war god. His arms are folded, his stance carved from discipline.

Paris — barely more than a boy — sits on the edge of his bed. The scent of rose oil still clings to him. His hands twitch. Guilt and defiance war across his face, each refusing to yield.

"This is a grievous predicament you have befallen us," Priam seethes, each word cold and sharpened. "A duel you demanded and fled. What madness caused such cowardice?"

His voice is not raised — he does not need to shout. The disappointment, the danger, is weight enough.

"You have invited the wrath of Sparta to our gates."

Paris lifts his chin, though it trembles. "I just could not bear... Facing death? Not before her. Not like that."

Hector's glare is a blade unsheathed. "Perhaps you should have considered this before sparking this war."

"I would have been butchered," Paris snaps, though even he doesn't seem to believe his own defense.

Hector's voice turns colder than bronze left in snow. "Better that than to live dishonored before Helen... and all of Troy."

The words slice. Paris rises in a quick breath, fists clenched. His brother takes a step forward — wrath ready to ignite.

"Enough."

Priam's word halts them both like a slammed shield. He raises his hand without turning. "Guard."

A soldier enters, face unreadable in the torchlight. Priam beckons Hector closer, murmuring something too low to catch. Hector nods — once — then sweeps from the room with the guard at his heels.

Now it is just father and son.

Priam's gaze lingers on the boy who has brought war between kingdoms for a woman's smile. On the prince who would not fight.

"The foe of my foe..." he murmurs, almost to himself, "may yet be our salvation."

And in the hour of war... they turned their gaze toward

us.

Meanwhile...

Far from Troy's golden towers, the land is quieter. Wilder.

The kingdom of Phthia basks in rugged solitude — a place of forests and iron-forged discipline. Here, the air is not scented with rose oil, but with sweat and soil and war.

Inside a modest stone dwelling, Odysseus stands like a shadow cast long by purpose. His eyes are sharp — always watching, always measuring. His tongue, as always, is armed with honey and poison both.

Across from him, Achilles leans against a post, bare-chested and silent. His skin gleams with the oil of training. His eyes — cold, patient, ancient despite youth — speak of blood spilled and legends forged before their time.

For we were known not for conquest... But for challenging those who claimed power unjustly.

"I have journeyed to Phthia on behalf of Sparta," Odysseus begins, his voice smooth as a river stone. "I implore you, Achilles. Join our ranks in battle against the Trojans. With you by our side, we shall know no defeat."

The silence stretches.

Achilles' eyes remain unmoved. He speaks with a calm that feels like thunder just over the horizon.

"And why would I bleed for Sparta?"

Odysseus doesn't flinch. "I bring with me troves of gifts. And promises. From the Spartan king."

For a moment, Achilles says nothing. Then — his jaw tightens. A grin breaks across his face, slow and cruel. Not joy. Not humor.

The grin of a man who has just seen a battlefield in his mind... and is already walking across it.

Golden light spills through lattice windows, bathing the high-ceilinged garden room in warmth. Dust motes drift in sunbeams like drifting pollen. Otrera stands still in the quiet, watching the morning unfold from the second story.

Below, the courtyard pulses with life. Ivy coils down ancient columns, vines hang thick with blossoms, and the stone beneath glistens from the dawn's dew.
In the center of it all, two young warriors crash together in a storm of wood and will.

Hippolyta — seventeen, all poise and precision — dances through each strike like she was born with sword in hand. Her movements are smooth, refined, dangerous.

Opposite her, Penthesilea — younger, smaller, but blazing with raw fire — presses forward, sweat streaking her brow, eyes sharp with purpose.

"You will not defeat me this time," she snarls, lunging.

But Hippolyta shifts aside like a breeze. With a single, practiced shove, Penthesilea crashes to the earth, the breath knocked from her lungs.

"It seems the fates still favor me, after all... sister," Hippolyta purrs, stepping over her without looking back. Laughter ripples from the rocks where Antiope and Melanippe sit — bruised, breathless, cheering like thunderclouds.

Penthesilea rises slowly, fingers brushing dirt from her palms. She doesn't look at her sisters. She looks up.

Otrera watches from the window, silent and glowing in the golden morning. Their eyes meet.

"   Victory always favors her," Penthesilea mutters, kicking a pebble with her heel.

Otrera smiles — not with pity, but with pride that flickers quiet and deep. "Remember," she calls out, "your story is just beginning. It will be yours soon enough."

Penthesilea sulks away, head low but jaw set. Otrera watches her go, her expression unreadable — except, perhaps, to the gods.

Footsteps echo in the hallway.

The queen turns as the doors open. In steps Hector, son of Priam — tall, regal, bearing the quiet power of those who've already lived too close to death.

Beside him walks Paleos — older, smaller, his eyes darting like a sparrow's. Behind them stand royal guards and one of Otrera's handmaidens.

The handmaiden bows, voice crisp.

"My Queen. Prince Hector and his escort, Paleos, come bearing word from King Priam."

Otrera's brow lifts. "King Priam?"

A nod.

Her lips press thin. "Very well."

Paleos steps forward, unfurling a scroll. He clears his throat as if preparing to recite an epic.

"Dearest Otrera, Queen of the Amazons. Your courage is legend. Your beauty... myth. The unspeakable indiscretions of my youngest son have brought war to our walls. We face ruin. And so, I send my son, Hector, in good faith, to ask for your aid. Should you agree, our debt shall be eternal."

The parchment curls at the ends. Silence folds in. Drawn by the sound of sparring, Hector drifts to the window.

Outside, the courtyard bursts with rhythm again. Hippolyta and Antiope clash in a spiral of speed. Melanippe dances barefoot atop a circle of stone, wild and radiant.

But Hector's eyes find another — quieter.

Penthesilea sits alone by a sun-warmed wall, surrounded by a halo of metal scraps, twine, and stones. Her fingers move swiftly, assembling something strange — like a bird trap or a broken weapon reimagined. She's focused. Unbothered.

She looks up. Their eyes meet across stone and silence.

Stillness settles.

"Are they yours?" Hector asks, voice hushed.

Otrera approaches the window, following his gaze.

"Yes," she says. "The two in battle are Hippolyta and Antiope. The free spirit is Melanippe. And that one there..."

She points.

"Penthesilea."

"Such a commanding name," Hector murmurs, "for someone so—"

"Small?" Otrera finishes with a raised brow.

"I was going to say beautiful."

Otrera laughs, soft and sharp. "Believe it or not, beauty is not her greatest virtue."

A flicker of something unreadable crosses Hector's face. He turns from the window, breath low.

"What message shall I carry to my father?"

Otrera does not hesitate. "Tell him... the Amazons will not choose sides. We have survived too much to gamble peace for pride."

After years spent hunted…

He nods. Disappointed. Respectful. He bows his head and exits with Paleos.

Mother vowed to never endanger our people again.

Alone once more, Otrera returns to the window. She hums, barely audible — a lullaby of old, the same she sang when firelight danced across a newborn's cheeks.

Below, Penthesilea frowns at her invention. She shifts a piece, tightens a coil. The thing buzzes, then breaks apart in her hands.

She sighs, undeterred.

CHAPTER 2

Themyscira — Spring, 1200 BCE

The sun crests over the cliffs — golden, gracious, unchallenged.

Its warmth spills onto the beaches below, where waves lap against the shore in quiet rhythm, frothing over sunlit stones. Beyond the sand, cliffs rise like sentinels — sharp-edged and pale — holding back forests thick with olive, laurel, and pine. Birds cry from the canopy. Citrus and salt ride the air. Themyscira breathes not just with life, but with legacy — an island ruled by women carved from war and wisdom.

At its heart, the Garden of Thermodon glows — orchids, red lilies, trumpet vines like fire spilled from stone. Bees hum lazily. The wind whispers of sacred things.

A single leaf spirals to the ground.

Then — chaos.

Footsteps hammer the forest floor. Twigs snap. Panting grows loud.

Penthesilea, once slight, now eighteen, barrels through the trees — breath hot in her throat, armor clinking with each step. Muscles firm, limbs long, her power still blooming into control. A bow thuds against her back. A shield grips her arm like a second skin.

To her left, Hippolyta. Her movements sleek and

sharpened with confidence. To her right, Antiope — fast, nimble, a blur in motion.

Hippolyta grins — fierce and taunting — then surges ahead.

Penthesilea snarls and pushes harder.

She leaps over a wall of branches, landing in a crouch. A doe watches from the clearing — startled, still.

Two wild things meet eyes.

The moment holds.

Then shatters.

The doe bolts. Penthesilea sprints.

The forest thins, spilling out onto sun-bleached sand.

The beach transforms into battleground — an obstacle course scrawled in brutality and brilliance. Wood, rope, stone, sweat. A crowd of Amazons roar at its edge. Bronze glints in the sun. Feathers sway in plumes. A few Gargareans — male warriors from a nearby settlement — watch in awe, wary yet enthralled.

At the course's end, twenty horses wait — sleek, strong, held by squires in white.

Hippolyta and Antiope break free first, vaulting onto their mounts in perfect rhythm.

Penthesilea bursts behind them. She throws herself onto a tall dun mare, hands sure on the reins.

"Hya!" she commands.

The horse obeys — fierce and fluid.

The forest spills more bodies into sunlight. The race ignites.

And watching it all — upon a white stallion that gleams like moonstone — is Otrera.

Queen.

Mother.

Warrior.

Her gaze sweeps the chaos — impassive, measured. Her circlet glints gold. Her shoulders are squared with purpose. She watches not for performance… but for promise.

"What a glorious day for sport," she murmurs.

Beside her, leaning on her stallion, Agius — rotund, flushed — nods with wine-stained lips.

"You must be proud, my queen."

"I am indeed," she replies.

But her gaze drifts skyward.

A shadow slips across her vision—a winged horse soaring overhead, its wings cutting the light in silence. She narrows her eyes, watching as it vanishes into the clouds. Below, a sharp neigh draws her attention.

Melanippe, youngest of the four sisters, stumbles from the tree line. Mud cakes her arms, twigs cling to her hair. She scrambles onto the last horse, nearly slipping from the saddle before righting herself.

Agius chuckles.

"Three of four is not bad."

Otrera kicks the stallion into a trot, leaving Agius without support. He crashes to the groud.

The first challenge: archery.

Hippolyta and Antiope draw in perfect unison,

their bows a mirrored motion of grace and ease.

Thwap. Thwap.

Twin arrows hit dead center. Bullseyes.

They vault from their horses, rolling across the sand. Amazon warriors in plumed helms rush to meet them, blades drawn. Wooden swords clash.

Penthesilea approaches fast. She draws her bow but falters—the edge of her breastplate pinches her arm, pushing the string off center. She breathes hard. Adjusts. Fires.

The arrow lands just shy of the center ring.

She doesn't flinch.

She leaps down, rolls, and draws her sword.

The waiting Amazon lunges. Penthesilea disarms her with brutal speed. The crowd gasps.

But the delay has cost her.

Hippolyta edges across the finish line first, only a heartbeat ahead of Antiope.

Penthesilea finishes third, barely a step behind.

Cheers erupt.

A wave of celebration rises for Hippolyta, who lifts her hands in mock humility. Antiope grins and claps her on the back.

Penthesilea pulls off her helmet and slams it into the sand.

Her beauty is striking—flushed cheeks, sharp jaw— but it is marred by tears brimming in her eyes.

Thyra bounds toward her, spear in hand, beaming.

"That was such a riveting display of sport!"

She wraps her arms around Penthesilea.

Penthesilea shoves her away. She rips the spear from Thyra's grasp, her hand shaking.

Thyra stumbles back, her joy fading into embarrassed stillness.

Hippolyta turns her back to them, laughing softly with Antiope.

Penthesilea hurls the spear.

It slices the air and lands just inches from Hippolyta's shoulder, buried in the sand.

Gasps ripple through the crowd. Silence falls like a storm cloud.

Hippolyta turns, unfazed. She smirks.

"Your aim offends the gods."

Penthesilea trembles now. Her breath is sharp. Her face burns.

"Do you think the spear strayed by accident?"

Hippolyta lifts her brows.

"Grace has never suited you in loss."

Penthesilea steps forward, eyes blazing. She tears off her breastplate, revealing a larger-than-average chest—the armor had never fit her properly. Her chest heaves.

"Come now," she growls. "Here and now. Blade to blade and I will show you what *sad* truly looks like."

Antiope steps forward, ready to intervene.

Hippolyta lifts a hand.

They stand chest to chest. Fury swirls between them, hot and unspoken.

Then—

"Enough."

Otrera rides between them, gaze cold and regal.

"Why must you quarrel like this? You are born of the same womb. It is time you honor that."

She looks at each of them in turn.

"You were born to lead. Lead well."

Neither moves.

"There may come a day when you will only have one another. What then?"

Silence.

Hippolyta exhales. Her pride softens, but only just.

"Mother is right."

She extends her hand.

Penthesilea stares at it. Her jaw clenches. Her fists tighten.

"Penthesilea," Otrera says.

Still nothing.

Hippolyta scoffs.

"Fine."

She turns, walking off with Antiope at her side.

Penthesilea remains, alone in the sand, her face tight with rage and shame.

Otrera dismounts and approaches.

"My darling daughter," she says gently, placing her hands on Penthesilea's shoulders. "You are blessed with so much potential."

Penthesilea doesn't answer. Her throat moves, but no sound comes.

"No one will ever question your heart," Otrera

continues. "But when you are defeated, you must do so honorably. As you would if you had crossed first."

Penthesilea's voice cracks.

"But when will I become the warrior you spoke of when I was a child?"

Otrera smiles sadly.

"I know the burden of wanting something so badly that you cannot see beyond the now. But... we all have our lessons to learn."

She pauses, her voice quieter now.

"Once you discover what those lessons are for you, only then will you fully flourish. Only then will you become all you were born to be."

A tear slips down Penthesilea's cheek. Her shoulders fall. The fire in her softens—but does not die.

"Now," Otrera says, brushing her daughter's hair from her eyes. "Retrieve your helmet. And celebrate. You are a warrior now."

Penthesilea nods. Turns. Walks slowly toward her discarded gear.

Elsewhere, at the tree line, Melanippe finally emerges.

She's filthy. Dazed. Mud stains her robes. Her hair is tangled around a wilted flower.

She looks around the empty clearing, blinking at the echo of cheers now faded.

"Where is everyone?"

The sun climbs higher, painting Themyscira's coastline in gold. Salt stings the air. Wind stirs through the crowd of Amazons gathered in a wide circle around a raised wooden dais. Atop it, Queen Otrera stands tall in full regalia—her bronze breastplate polished to mirror-shine, her gaze steady and commanding.

Before her, lined in formation beneath the watching eyes of sisters, elders, and guests, stand the newest initiates. Hippolyta, fierce and still flushed from exertion. Antiope, chin high, proud. Penthesilea, shoulders squared, but her expression unreadable. Their armor catches the sun, gleaming like fire-kissed metal.

Otrera raises her arms.

"Behold…" Her voice carries like a sacred rite. "Our newest army initiates. True warriors."

Stillness.

Then the crowd erupts—cheers, applause, the clatter of fists on shields. A surge of pride courses through the spectators like a tide breaking.

"You have just completed one of the finest trials ever seen on this land."

More applause. Siblings rush forward with feathered helmets, placing them ceremonially atop the bowed heads of the initiates. Sand swirls at their feet. Some women weep. Others holler in celebration.

From the corner of her eye, Hippolyta glances down the line. Her face is sharp with victory—eyes aglow, lips curled into a faint smirk. She seeks Penthesilea.

But Penthesilea remains still, her face unmoving, as

though carved from stone. Her hands stay clenched at her sides. Her helmet is accepted with silent reluctance.

"And I do not say this out of favoritism," Otrera continues, sweeping the crowd with her gaze. "Not even for my own."

Hippolyta and Antiope exchange a knowing look, their bond reaffirmed in triumph.

But Penthesilea's eyes shift, catching something the others don't. At the edge of the circle, Melanippe stands alone. Her shoulders slump. Her head lowers as Otrera speaks again.

"Those among you who did not complete the course with adequacy shall partake in the ritual tonight."

Melanippe bows her head and disappears into the crowd, slipping away in silence. No one notices her absence—except Penthesilea.

Otrera steps down from the platform, her ceremonial sandals brushing sand from the edge.

Nearby, Antiope snickers.

"Melanippe, simply, was not born to battle. Perhaps born to breed?"

Penthesilea turns, voice clipped and cold. "She is still our sister."

Antiope doesn't flinch. "Is she?"

Their eyes lock, cold steel behind each glance. Then Penthesilea breaks it. She walks away, fury contained behind a taut jaw.

Antiope lifts her palms. "What?"

Otrera approaches then, brushing past Antiope.

"Hippolyta," she says, "come with me."

Without hesitation, Hippolyta steps forward. They pass Penthesilea, who now stands beside Thyra, waiting in the sand.

Penthesilea draws a slow breath.

"Thyra," she says softly, "I offer many apologies. My behavior earlier was not honorable."

Thyra tilts her head, curious.

"You did not deserve such a poor display of sportsmanship," Penthesilea continues. "My sister… she always prevails, and it stirs something within—"

Thyra reaches up, brushing the curve of Penthesilea's cheek with the back of her fingers.

"I am well aware of your competitive spirit," she says with a faint, amused smile. "I took no offense."

Penthesilea gently takes her hand, presses her lips to it.

"How fortunate I am."

Thyra laughs quietly, and the two walk off, hand in hand, the tension of the morning easing between them.

A chamber carved into the ancient rock beneath Themyscira—cool, sacred, and dimly lit by the flicker of torchlight. The air smells of soot and old salt. Relics line the room: gilded swords, weathered shields, ceremonial armor once worn by warrior queens long buried. Bronze and gold gleam softly in the stillness.

At the room's heart lies a simple leather girdle, set atop a black pedestal, unassuming among the finery.

Hippolyta enters first. Her eyes widen as she takes it all in. Her voice is reverent.

"The artistry. So captivating."

Otrera follows at her side.

"After today," she says, "it is time you knew of this gift. Left by your father."

Hippolyta glances at the girdle, brow raised.

"It holds a power unlike any other," Otrera continues. "So coveted, many have tried to steal it from this very room."

She lifts the protective glass with practiced care and removes the girdle, the leather worn but strong.

She turns, offering it.

"All of this beauty…" Hippolyta says, skeptical, "and this is what he left me?"

Otrera smiles.

"Oh, my child. There is far more to it than meets the eye."

Hippolyta accepts the belt, her fingers tightening around it. It is heavier than it looks.

"Careful," Otrera warns gently.

"What power does it bear?" Hippolyta asks.

"Try it on."

Intrigued, Hippolyta nods. Otrera steps forward, carefully wrapping the girdle around her daughter's waist.

The moment the clasp fastens, the air shifts.

The belt flickers—then glows. Threads of golden light trace up Hippolyta's spine, radiating across her skin like veins of sunlight. Her eyes widen as the glow pulses outward, surging like breath through her limbs.

She steps toward a massive block of carved stone, hesitating only for a moment.

Then, with one hand, she lifts it.

It rises from the floor like paper, effortless in her grip.

Otrera watches, solemn and proud.

"Now," she says, "you see."

"The strength," Hippolyta breathes.

"So much," Otrera murmurs, "harnessed in something so simple. So small."

Hippolyta sets the stone down gently, gaze still fixed on the girdle.

"That is enough for now," Otrera says, reaching to unfasten it.

The golden light dims. The belt returns to leather and thread, aged and ordinary.

"Astonishing."

"It will not be long before you take the throne," Otrera says. "Until then, the belt remains here."

She replaces it in its glass case with care, as if returning fire to the hearth.

Hippolyta lingers, staring a moment longer, the weight of future crowns beginning to settle on her brow.

Chapter 3

The hill-fort of Tiryns glows like an ember beneath the setting sun. Built into the rock and crowned with walls so thick they seem to grow from the stone itself, the citadel hums with life. Oil lamps flicker in the gathering dusk, casting long shadows across weathered stone. Merchants shout over one another in the lower markets, peddling bronze trinkets, salted meats, and imported silks. Servants rush between gates, while soldiers lounge against archways, spears cradled in idle hands.

Through the bustle, a lone rider cuts through the noise.

The crowd parts instinctively, drawn either by his sheer size or something primal in his presence. A man of towering breadth, he commands not just his own steed, but four monstrous horses trailing behind him on taut ropes. Their hides are glossy with sweat, their eyes still wide with bloodlust. These are the Mares of Diomedes—flesh-eaters, untamable beasts—yet they move now with the submission of animals broken by the hand of a god.

Inside the great hall—The Megaron—of the fortress, wine flows and meat steams from clay platters as two dozen warriors revel. The vaulted chamber rings with boisterous chatter, crude songs, and the guttural laughter of men half-drunk on barley ale.

Two warriors wrestle over the last haunch of lamb, their scuffle drawing cheers. A jug topples. Wine splashes across the marble floor. Someone begins to drum on his plate.

Then—a fist crashes into the table.

The sound is thunderous.

A hush swallows the room whole. The meat wrestlers freeze mid-struggle. Cups halt midair. All heads turn toward the vast doorway, now filled by a single figure.

He does not need to raise his voice.

"Enough."

The word slices through the silence like a blade. Without hesitation, every man drops to his knees.

"Hail the king," they murmur in unison.

King Eurystheus steps into the hall, flanked by guards clad in embossed bronze. His frame is thick, his golden armor ostentatious, glinting in the firelight. His brow is broad, but the eyes beneath are cold and calculating. Every motion he makes is slow and theatrical, intended to remind all who watch who commands the land beneath their feet.

He surveys the chaos, expression sour.

"Out. All of you."

The warriors scramble, falling over one another in their haste. One man snatches the disputed lamb haunch as he flees, stuffing it into his cloak.

Eurystheus watches with a faint smile that vanishes the moment their backs are turned.

A portly man wrapped in fine wool and gold clasps waddles through the silent chamber, sandals slapping against the stone. He clutches a scroll tight to his chest as though it holds the words of the Fates themselves.

At the feet of King Eurystheus, he bows low, then drops to both knees with a grunt.

"Hail, King Eurystheus," he gasps.

The king barely nods. A flick of his fingers.

The messenger scrambles upright. His face is red, glistening with sweat.

"Heracles has returned."

Eurystheus's lips curl—just slightly.

"Very well," he says. "Send him in."

The man hurries out, breath catching as he vanishes down the hall.

A moment passes.

Then the door creaks open.

Heracles enters.

He fills the space like a statue come to life—taller than any man in the court, his shoulders wide enough to blot the light behind him. His chestplate is dented and scorched, and over it drapes a lion's pelt, its great head still snarling in death. His beard is thick, his face smudged with dust and dried blood.

Behind him, the mares snort and paw the floor, tugging at the ropes that bind them.

Eurystheus doesn't rise. His voice tightens through clenched teeth.

"Dear cousin. You made it back in one piece."

Heracles offers a half-smile.

"Surely that was your wish, Eurystheus."

"Contrarily. I dare not expect anything less from the son of Zeus."

The king steps forward, approaching the mares. He circles them like a man admiring artwork, though his eyes betray unease. They do not rear. They do not bite. Their muzzles are stained red, but their heads are lowered, subdued.

"They say the Mares of Diomedes feast on the flesh of men," he murmurs. "That they cannot be mastered."

He runs a hand along one of their necks. The beast doesn't flinch.

"And yet here they stand as calm as a house dog. And you… unscathed."

Heracles shrugs the leather satchel from his shoulder. It lands on the marble with a thick, wet thump. From its mouth rolls a severed foot—gnawed, half-eaten, the bone stripped to the marrow.

"Diomedes fed them well," Heracles says.

The king's face twitches. He waves to a guard, who rushes to collect the reins and lead the animals away with careful, trembling hands.

Eurystheus returns to his throne.

He lounges into it with theatrical nonchalance, drumming his fingers on the armrest.

"Impressive," he says. "Overcoming the most fearsome… The Nemean lion."

His gaze flicks to the pelt slung over Heracles' back.

"The Stymphalian Birds. The Erymanthian Boar. Even the Cretan Bull."

Heracles stands motionless.

"Failure is not permitted me."

"Ah yes," the king says, voice like a drawn dagger. "Atonement. For the blood you spilled of your own kin."

The words hang there, heavy.

Heracles' jaw tightens.

"Twelve years of tasks will not restore them. But they may spare me damnation."

Eurystheus leans forward, voice low and coiled with satisfaction.

"So be it. Your next labor… Fetch the belt of Hippolyta."

Heracles raises a brow.

"You would have me journey to Themyscira… for a belt?"

"Not a belt," Eurystheus says softly. "A sacred gift from Ares himself. And I desire it."

Heracles considers him. The silence crackles with ancient bloodlines and unspoken hatred.

"As you wish."

Without another word, he turns and walks toward the door.

The king watches him go, his fingers white around the edge of his throne. Beneath the gold and pomp, something colder glimmers in his eyes.

Not admiration.

But fear.

Chapter 4

The sea churns beneath a hazy pink sky, waves curling toward the shore like restless thoughts. Penthesilea sits near the tide's reach, a figure of solitude and simmering reflection. One by one, she hurls stones into the water—sharp, fast, and final, as if daring the ocean to hurl them back.

Hippolyta approaches in silence, her shadow stretching long beside her sister. She watches the horizon before speaking.

"Curious how the churning sea soothes a restless soul," she says, her voice low, contemplative. "One might expect the opposite."

She looks down at Penthesilea.

"What troubles you, Sister?"

Penthesilea doesn't meet her gaze. Another stone sails from her fingers.

"Must there always be something? Can I not enjoy the view in peace?"

Hippolyta lowers herself beside her. The silence folds over them—for a moment, almost comfortable.

"I have known your first breath," she says gently. "I know when something weighs you down."

The sea rumbles, swallowing her words.

Penthesilea sighs. Her voice comes after a long pause.

"I train harder than anyone. Even harder than you. But no matter how far I push myself… you always win." She bites the words before they can soften.

"I'll never escape your shadow. It will always be you they see first."

Hippolyta listens. When she responds, her voice is calm, thoughtful.

"Penthesilea, I never meant to diminish you. Even as children… I only wanted to push you. I still do."

Penthesilea scoffs faintly.

"You think you bear no flaws?"

"I command respect," Hippolyta replies, "but only because it is earned. And you will too. Not through appearances—but through your fire."

She pauses, her tone softening.

"A fire I have only seen in our mother. In time, I dare say… your light will outshine us all."

She draws Penthesilea into a quiet embrace—sisters not at war, but at peace, if only for a moment.

Then, she leans back.

"Shall we go? The ceremony awaits."

Penthesilea nods. They rise together, shoulder to shoulder, the wind sweeping across the beach as if blessing their truce.

Night cloaks Themyscira in silver and shadow. In the Garden of Thermodon, a great fire roars, casting light across stone paths and wildflowers. Smoke curls upward into the stars. Amazons and a few visiting

Gargareans gather in loose circles—some laughing, some whispering, some tangled in silent, smoldering contact beneath the veil of ritual.

Hippolyta and Antiope sit apart from the revelry, quiet in their observations.

"It is a bitter thing, needing men to endure," Antiope mutters.

"Well, sister…" Hippolyta gestures toward the entangled bodies by the fire. "At least we are spared from…"

She trails off with a vague wave.

Antiope raises an imaginary cup.

"To that, I raise my blade. I'd rather slay them all."

Melanippe drops beside them, her curls tousled, her tunic wrinkled.

"Ah. The zeal of one who's never been touched."

Antiope turns slowly.

"And you have?"

A soft grin spreads across Melanippe's face.

"How noble of you," Antiope retorts.

"On the contrary… they can serve a purpose. Pleasurable. Relieving."

Antiope shrugs, eyes on the fire.

"No, thank you. I enjoy my pent-up rage."

Hippolyta chuckles.

"Other than vengeance, there is no better fuel."

Melanippe nods with mock reverence.

"And that is why you're both so terrifying."

Antiope scans the crowd.

"Speaking of rage… where is Penthesilea?"

Alone in her quarters, Penthesilea lies submerged in warm water, the tub carved from a single slab of dark stone. Steam coils upward like memory. She hums an old lullaby—soft, hollow, almost a whisper. The song drifts like incense, too faint to rouse anything but ghosts.

The door creaks.

Thyra enters with a tray. The moment shifts.

Penthesilea stops humming. Her arms wrap over her chest, instinctively guarded.

"That song… it was lovely," Thyra says.

"Our mother sang it to us as children."

"I have never heard you hum it before."

"Really?"

Thyra sets the tray down gently. The air thickens with something unspoken.

"Do not hide. Your scars—wear them. They speak to the warrior you are."

She kneels beside the tub.

"I have always found you beautiful. But when I cared for you… I saw more."

She lifts a cloth and begins to bathe Penthesilea with reverence.

"There's no beauty greater than passion."

Their eyes meet. The stillness tightens.

A bonfire blazes in the Garden of Thermodon, flames reaching into the night. Around it, shadows sway—

Amazons and Gargareans in laughter and longing. Some slip into shadowed paths, their laughter dissolving into breathless whispers. The air simmers with the heat of want —of youth, survival, and closeness earned.

Steam rises from a marble basin elsewhere. Penthesilea stands, water streaming from her form. Her breath is steady, her body honed and marked by time. Thyra waits with a cloth. She steps forward, wrapping her queen, hands brushing up her sides—slow, reverent.

Penthesilea catches her wrists, deliberate and warm. She brings Thyra's palms to her lips, kisses them like a vow, then traces her mouth along her arm. She stops just short of her lips. A breath, held between them.

Then—a kiss. Not lustful. Tender. A quiet ache, a promise whispered in skin.

Far below, the sacred vault hums.

Hippolyta returns alone, footsteps echoing between ancient walls. Her eyes fall on the leather girdle beneath its dome. She steps forward, removes it, and binds it to her waist.

The clasp clicks.

Light bursts forth—not flame, but something divine. Gold and white surge through her, illuminating her from within. She catches her breath. In that instant, she is more than flesh—she is legend, manifest.

On the moonlit shore, Otrera walks barefoot. The

tide brushes her ankles, the sea hushed like a prayer. Her face is unreadable—timeless—but her gaze stretches beyond the waves.

In the quiet chamber, Penthesilea and Thyra lie entwined. Firelight flickers across their skin. Thyra's fingers trace Penthesilea's scars—over ribs, hips, and collarbones healed long ago. To her, they are not flaws, but scripture.

She drifts lower, fingers grazing soft skin—

Penthesilea stops her, gently. Not tonight.

Then, with fluid grace, she moves above her. Her arms brace the space between them. Her mouth finds Thyra's neck, breath steady, reverent. Thyra exhales—not in surrender, but in communion.

This is not conquest.

It is presence.

Intimacy, unarmored.

Hippolyta roams the sacred chamber, belt aglow, blade drawn. She moves with fluid precision—a goddess wrapped in steel. With a flick, she topples a marble stand. Not in anger. In indifference. Let it fall.

Above, a sudden neigh splits the silence.

Otrera halts, gaze skyward.

There—against the moon—a winged horse, shadowed and radiant, rider haloed in starlight.

The ocean answers in thunder.

Otrera steps back.

Behind her, a streak of light tears through the sky—
a falling star, gone in a breath.

The world holds its breath.

Then the wind returns.

And the fire keeps burning.

CHAPTER 5

The chamber rests beneath the soft hush of midnight.

Moonlight spills through sheer linen draped over tall, narrow windows, casting drifting patterns across the stone floor—shapes that sway with the rhythm of the ocean wind. The air holds the faint scent of lavender and salt—crushed petals clinging to linen, the sea's memory carried in on the wind. Cool marble breathes beneath them, softened only by woven mats and layers of silk across the bedding platform.

Penthesilea lies beneath a spill of linens, her skin glowing faintly in the silver light, limbs entangled with Thyra's. Their bodies press close, not with urgency, but in a gentle tangle of trust and heat, like vines wrapping one another in lazy, inevitable coils. Fingers trace skin in slow, idle circles—movements unhurried, unspoken, the kind born of familiarity and longing stitched together.

Thyra speaks first, her voice no louder than a thought, each word trailing the scent of sleep and embers.

"I long to return the joy you bestow upon me."

Penthesilea's lips quirk into a half-smile, part defiance, part surrender.

"Rules are rules," she murmurs, though the words carry little weight. A pause, soft and aching.

"But I concede... Staying pure grows harder each

time I am near you."

Their eyes meet, a silent exchange stretched longer than time allows, carrying more tenderness than words can hold. A smile flickers—wry, wistful, quietly knowing.

Then—a knock.

Not loud, but firm—enough to shift the air between them.

Thyra's fingers pause. The moonlight tenses.

"Oh. Sister? Are you in there?"

Antiope's voice filters through the door—amused, unmistakable.

Footsteps follow—the confident stride of someone who never questions her right to enter. Around the carved stone doorway, Antiope appears: tall and proud, dark hair tied back for movement, bow slung casually over one shoulder. Her smirk arrives before her words.

"Thought I might find you here with your maiden," she says, sarcasm warm rather than cruel.

Penthesilea reacts with practiced ease, sweeping a thin coverlet over herself and Thyra with soldier-swiftness.

"What is it you seek?" she asks, her voice level again, though her pulse hums beneath her ribs.

Antiope steps farther in, letting corridor torchlight cast sharp lines across her cheekbones.

"Thought it a fine time for a bit of... exertion," she says, pausing to let the word linger. Her gaze shifts toward the open window, where the sea breeze whispers of unrest.

"You never turn down training," she adds. "One of the few things we both still honor."

Penthesilea exhales quietly.

"Was the challenge of this morning not enough?

Antiope shrugs, effortless.

"With all this repressed energy—"

"Say no more."

Penthesilea turns to Thyra with a nod, a small smile —a silent vow that this moment is not lost, only paused. Then she rises, silk slipping from her like water down polished stone. She is every inch a queen. And a warrior.

The forest yawns wide beneath a pale, watchful moon.

A clearing stretches open like a secret kept by trees. The air is thick with pine and loam, and the quiet hum of unseen life pulses beneath the underbrush. Cloth targets hang from ancient oaks in a rough arc, their fabric frayed by hundreds of arrows past. Beneath them, thick branches lie stacked—warped, darkened with sweat, worn smooth by time. Primitive weights for a regiment forged in strength.

Two parallel tracks stretch away from the clearing, each fifty yards long and disappearing into the shadows of deeper woods. Moonlight glints on every leaf as though the gods themselves had touched them.

Penthesilea and Antiope step into this sacred space, boots quiet on packed earth. Bows and quivers slung at their backs, waterskins brushing against their hips. They move with quiet purpose—fluid, unspoken. Their breathing syncs without instruction.

"You have been busy," Penthesilea notes, scanning the arrangement—admiration faint, but present.

Antiope grins.

"All fire and no place to burn it. Shall we?"

They drop their gear at the first marker and jog to the far end of the path. The forest stills.

"Three... Two... One."

They launch.

The sprint is fierce and clean. Bodies surge into motion, arms pumping, breath sharp and steady. Penthesilea edges ahead by a hair—her stride powerful, precise. Antiope follows close, relentless.

At the far end, they drop to the branches without slowing.

Down. Lift. Down again.

Ten reps. Muscles strain and flex, shaped by ritual and resilience. Penthesilea finishes a half-breath ahead, already pivoting into a crouch. Her fingers close around her bow, smooth and certain.

Arrows whistle through the air.

Penthesilea looses one—then another. Both strike the hanging cloth. Sharp, pulsing thuds.

Antiope's shot splits the center of her target—clean, decisive.

Penthesilea's final arrow veers slightly. She grits her teeth, takes a moment longer, bowstring taut with hesitation.

A moment too long.

Antiope bolts. Her legs churn into the second

sprint, vanishing down the path before Penthesilea reacts. When she does, the lead is already lost.

At the finish, Antiope sips lazily from her waterskin. She doesn't gloat—just breathes, flushed with victory.

Penthesilea arrives moments later, chest heaving, breath hot.

She says nothing. Instead, she stalks toward a nearby boulder and slams it to the ground with sudden, brutal force.

A wet crunch.

A rat, hidden in the grass, crushed beneath the stone. It twitches violently—spasms—then slumps, broken but not yet dead.

Antiope watches the outburst with cool amusement.

"Why so troubled, sister? Detest defeat?"

Penthesilea wipes sweat from her brow. Her voice is low, clipped.

"Do not start, Antiope."

Antiope raises both hands.

"I would not dare dream of it. I respect your competitive spirit."

She pauses, letting silence settle.

"We are of the same ilk, you and I."

The words fall like ash between them.

Penthesilea drinks. Cool water cuts through the heat in her blood.

"Hippolyta, though..." Antiope starts, slower now.

"She acts the warrior, but deep down—"

"She is more leader than fighter," Penthesilea interrupts—not harsh, but resolute.

Antiope nods once.

"Yes. Perhaps the burden of being firstborn."

"Perhaps."

Antiope tosses her waterskin to the ground.

"Anyway... I just let her win."

Penthesilea turns her head, narrowing her eyes.

"You do not?" She quips.

Antiope grins, the edges of her smile curling like smoke.

"Reset and go again?" she offers.

Penthesilea's smirk returns—half-worn, half-eager.

"I dare not have it any other way."

Without ceremony, Antiope slings an arm over her sister's shoulders. They turn and walk back toward the center of the clearing. Leaves shift beneath their feet, soft and even.

Then—from above—a cry.

Piercing. High. Sharp as a blade drawn across bone.

A vulture's call. Distant, but clear.

It slices through the stillness like an omen whispered from the gods.

Behind them, where the boulder rests sunken in the earth, the rat gives a final twitch—a shallow shudder—

And then, silence.

CHAPTER 6

The Garden of Thermodon glows in the blush of morning. Dew clings to each petal and leaf, glimmering like tiny pearls strewn across a canvas of color. Vines curl around pale stone columns. Wildflowers stretch toward the warming sun. The earth seems to breathe, slow and content.

Otrera walks barefoot through it all, the grass cool beneath her feet. Her fingers brush tall ferns and golden blossoms. The breeze is gentle, scented with mint and thyme. Butterflies drift through shafts of sunlight, their wings whispering against the air.

She reaches a familiar stack of smooth, timeworn stones and lowers herself onto them, folding into quiet stillness. Her eyes close. She breathes deeply.

Peace dwells here.

Then—the light falters.

Clouds gather, casting gray over gold. The butterflies vanish.

A silence falls. Not a natural quiet, but the kind that arrives before something ancient stirs.

From the crevices of the earth, spiders begin to emerge. First a handful. Then dozens. Then hundreds. They scurry silently over her feet, up the stones, and across her skin. Tiny legs skitter along her calves, her thighs.

Otrera remains motionless. Her breath shallows.

A hiss slithers through the garden. It comes from nowhere—and from everywhere.

Above, vultures spiral in slow, widening arcs. Their shrill cries pierce the stillness, approaching.

The spiders reach her arms.

Dread thickens like fog.

She stands slowly, arms rising skyward, a call lifted to the heavens.

"Gods of Olympia... what is this omen?"

A horse's cry breaks the air—sharp, unmistakable.

Otrera lifts her gaze.

A shadow slices across the clouds, swift and silent. Wind tousles her hair.

Her body freezes.

The city–Otrera's home from long ago–burned beneath a bloodless moon.

A whistle cut the air. Then groans. Then screams. Footsteps pounding. Steel clashing. Fire licking the rooftops.

Otrera thundered through the chaos, torchlight dancing off her blade. All around her, women fled with their daughters, battered and desperate—gripping weapons, dragging the wounded, crying for freedom. Fire clawed up the stone walls.

She saw him.

A boy. Bellerophon. Small, alone, no older than five. Standing in the doorway of a crumbling home. His face was streaked with soot and tears, a sharp scar etched beneath his right eye. He reached for her.

Otrera's horse did not slow.

She looked back—once.

Then the memory shattered.

Otrera gasps back into the present. She is still upon
the stones. The garden now colder. The wind—harsher.

Her eyes sweep the horizon.

There, far off, a shape descends from the clouds.

A winged horse.

It cuts through the sky like a blade.

Otrera turns. She runs.

Elsewhere...

On the cliffs where the sea meets sky, Melanippe
sits in peaceful poise. The ocean stretches wide and
glittering. Beside her, a woven basket brims with pink and
blue anemones. Their petals tremble softly in the wind.

With slow care, she selects a pink blossom and
braids it into her dark hair, each motion tender, precise—
like a prayer.

Hoofbeats echo behind her.

Antiope arrives on horseback, her shield strapped
to her back, sword flashing in the sun. She dismounts and
strides forward.

"Must you waste time with flowers and
daydreams?" she says, disapproving. "You should be
training."

Melanippe doesn't flinch. She ties off the braid with

quiet grace.

"Daydreams will not stop an arrow," Antiope presses.

"No," Melanippe replies, finally turning. Her voice is calm, her expression unshaken. "But they bring light. And love. Are those not worth defending too? Is training more noble than nurturing your heart?"

Antiope's mouth hardens, but her tone softens.

"You are too naive. There will always be war."

She reaches out, brushing a finger against the edge of the braid.

"Anemones," Melanippe murmurs.

"What?"

"The flowers. Each color has meaning—birth, life, death, spirit. Pink means love and care. It's my favorite."

Antiope withdraws her hand.

"You're the daughter of warriors. Surely your hands are meant for more than weaving."

She scoffs.

"If only you channeled all this into combat."

Melanippe's smile is soft, undeterred.

"If only you let joy in as fiercely as you embrace war. Balance is the strongest shield."

Antiope stares. Beneath Melanippe's calm lies something unmovable. Ancient. The fighter in Antiope wants to refute it—but the sister hesitates.

Melanippe reaches out and takes her hand.

"Let me show you how to braid your hair. Perhaps then, you'll feel what I feel."

Antiope nearly laughs.
But she sits beside her.
Melanippe plucks a pink anemone from the basket.
And they begin.

CHAPTER 7

The forest is alive with the gentle murmur of dawn. Birds chirp in rhythmic patterns overhead, their music drifting through a canopy painted with golden light. Wildflowers bloom in careless clusters, their colors bright against the soft green undergrowth, as if the gods themselves had scattered them in celebration of the new day.

Penthesilea lies still among the tall grass, her limbs draped across the forest floor like a warrior fallen at rest. She stirs. Her lashes flutter. A yawn escapes her lips as her muscles stretch and unknot, reluctant to leave the comfort of sleep. The trials of the previous night still cling to her skin like mist.

A sudden crack of a twig—a sharp, jarring sound—shatters the stillness.

Her eyes snap toward the source. In one breath, she's upright, reaching for the sword lying a few strides away. Her hand closes around the hilt with trained precision.

"Who goes there?"

Her voice is firm, low. Her eyes sweep the trees, muscles tight with readiness.

From the brush, a familiar figure emerges. Thyra steps into the light, serene and unhurried, a small woven basket brimming with wild herbs and blooms tucked in the crook of her arm. Her bare feet make no sound against the soft earth.

"What brings you here?" Penthesilea asks, posture easing though her breath still holds tension.

"I came looking for you," Thyra says gently.

Penthesilea brushes soil from her tunic, steadying herself. Thyra stops a few paces away, her voice quiet with concern.

"You were not beside me when I woke."

"I only meant to rest a while," Penthesilea replies, a faint smile touching her lips. "My eyelids proved heavier than expected."

"When are they not?"

The corner of Penthesilea's mouth lifts. A brief but real laugh slips from her. The tension begins to ease from her frame.

"What are you gathering?" she asks, eyeing the basket.

"Herbs and flowers. You can—"

Before Thyra can finish, Penthesilea closes the distance and plants a kiss on her cheek, light and fleeting. Thyra's eyes brighten with quiet intimacy.

"How was last night? With Antiope?"

Penthesilea walks to where her bow and quiver rest beside a patch of flattened grass. She bends, fingers tracing the worn leather.

"I prevailed in two of... twelve."

"Twelve?" Thyra teases. "I now understand the reason for your weariness."

Penthesilea's voice dips. "I fear I'm not enough. I fall short... again and again. I fear I will never be as great as Hippolyta or Antiope."

Thyra steps close. Her hands rise and gently cup Penthesilea's face, thumbs grazing the warrior's cheeks as if grounding her.

"You are enough. More than enough."

She moves one hand to rest over Penthesilea's heart.

"You carry a kind heart and a fierce spirit. That is what makes you extraordinary."

Penthesilea's shoulders soften beneath the weight of those words. Her hand comes up to hold Thyra's, and for a moment, she forgets everything else.

"Thank you, Thyra. You unfailingly bring warmth to my heart."

Thyra grins and nudges her shoulder playfully against Penthesilea's, their familiarity unspoken but deeply felt.

"Is that not what friends are for?"

Penthesilea raises an eyebrow with a wry smirk. "Friends, indeed?"

She teases the hem of Thyra's dress before they begin walking, steps falling into sync, surrounded by the quiet rustle of leaves.

"Do you remember the time when I tried my hand at that healing elixir... and my hair turned green?"

"How could I not? You looked like a forest nymph for weeks."

A distant neigh slices through the calm. They both stop.

A massive shadow glides silently across the moss-covered ground. They look up. Through the trees, a winged horse drifts across the sky like a myth in motion. Penthesilea's eyes narrow, wary.

A sharp, distant neigh cleaves the air — high, urgent, and unlike any creature native to the forest. Penthesilea and Thyra freeze. The sound hangs between them like a curse, unnatural in its clarity, cutting through the leaves and branches as if the trees themselves are listening.

A shadow unfurls across the forest floor. It glides past their feet like a passing storm cloud, vast and winged.

They lift their heads.

Above, glimpsed through the trembling canopy, a white, winged horse glides silently across the moonlight—its enormous wings slicing the air in perfect rhythm, too graceful, too ominous. The beast carries the weight of something divine and war-bound. Penthesilea narrows her gaze. Her brow creases, instinct warning her before thought catches up. Something is coming.

Then the earth groans.

A deep, distant boom shakes the ground. The trees creak. Birds scatter from their branches in a rush of flapping wings. The tremor rolls beneath their feet, low and slow at first, like a heartbeat beneath the soil.

Penthesilea stiffens. "What the…"

A second boom erupts—louder this time. Closer.

The tremor becomes a quake, and the ground lurches beneath them with an audible shudder. Tree roots groan. Stones clatter.

She reacts instantly, pure instinct. Penthesilea throws an arm across Thyra and shoves her back, out of the clearing, toward the dense cover of the garden paths.

"Go."

Thyra doesn't move. "Not without you."

"You will be safer in the garden. I will be fine. I promise." A pause. Her voice softens, urgent and unshakable. "Now, go."

Thyra falters for just a breath. Then she turns and runs, her dark form swallowed quickly by the trees.

Alone now, Penthesilea presses herself against a thick, ancient tree trunk, its bark gnarled and cold against her skin. Her breaths come light and shallow. All around her, the forest seems to lean inward.

Twigs snap in the distance—short, sharp, rapid. Then come the footsteps. Heavy. Relentless. A pounding rhythm growing closer, louder, like some great beast charging unseen.

She raises her bow and draws an arrow with practiced calm. Fingers wrap around the string. Her arm steadies. Her eyes scan left, then right, her aim slow and methodical. She does not blink. She waits.

Then—

The brush ahead bursts apart.

Otrera explodes into view, breath heaving, armor dented, hair wild, blood streaking her arms and thighs.

Behind her—just a heartbeat behind—a massive boulder crashes into the earth, missing her by inches. The impact sends up a spray of dirt and stone, tearing at the underbrush.

She keeps running, gasping for air, her feet pounding the earth. Another boom. Another stone slams down just where she had been, the ground cracking beneath it.

From above, faint but terrible, comes the cry of the winged horse again—shrill, proud, untouchable.

Otrera doesn't stop. She hacks at the brush with her sword, clearing her path with desperate, brutal swings. Branches snap and thorns tear at her skin. She dives headfirst into the hollow of a fallen tree, vanishing into its shadowed curve. Her breath comes in ragged bursts. Her hand trembles.

Something is coming. Fast.

A rustle rushes toward her—too quick, too close. Her eyes fly wide.

"Penthesilea."

With a surge of effort, Otrera launches from cover and hurls herself forward. She collides with Penthesilea just as another boulder falls from the sky and smashes into the earth behind them, spraying debris. The force of the dive sends Penthesilea sprawling to the ground. Her bow tumbles beside her, her quiver half-spilling across the mossy floor.

She scrambles up, unharmed, and turns.

Otrera doesn't rise.

The boulder—massive, slick, heavy as a small hill—pins her body to a patch of white anemones. The delicate flowers are crushed beneath the weight, their petals streaked and blooming with red. Blood seeps into the soft soil.

"Mother!" Penthesilea cries out, rushing to her mother, hands clawing at the rock, fingers digging into cracks. She grits her teeth and strains, shoulders flexing with all her might—but the boulder does not budge. It might as well be the earth itself.

Otrera's chest moves in shallow jerks. Her face is tight with pain. Blood clings to her lips.

"I need to get help," Penthesilea says, already half-standing, looking wildly into the trees for someone, anyone.

But Otrera's hand clamps around her wrist, firm despite the tremor in her fingers.

"No."

Penthesilea turns, eyes wide with alarm.

"But if I—"

"This is my fate," Otrera says, each word a struggle. "My death will bring peace between those who hunt us and our nation."

"You are not going to die. Not now. We just need to get this..." Penthesilea's eyes search the forest in desperation, but there is no one else. No help coming.

"My sweet daughter. Look at me."

She does.

Tears blur her vision. Her gaze locks on her

mother's face, and time stills.

Otrera reaches up and touches her cheek with a trembling hand.

"You possess great strength. A heart as bright and warm as the sun." She coughs, a horrible, rattling breath. "I have never been more proud."

Penthesilea clasps her mother's hand in both of hers, holding it tightly, her whole body trembling.

"My love for you will remain boundless for all eternity."

Then, slowly, Otrera releases her final breath. A long, soft exhale.

Stillness.

Penthesilea doesn't move. Her eyes fix on her mother's face, unmoving. Her expression twists—grief breaking through her in waves. She is not ready. There is no time for this.

A shift of light crosses the anemones. A shadow moves.

She looks up.

The winged horse circles high above, its rider silhouetted against the thinning clouds.

Her muscles snap to life. She rises, limbs shaking, jaw clenched. Her eyes burn. Her hands curl into fists.

And then—she runs.

Penthesilea bursts through the trees and into the clearing like a storm. Her bow is already in her hands, drawn tight. She looks up.

Above the treetops, radiant against the morning

sun, Pegasus soars—his wings wide, flawless, shining like polished ivory. His hooves do not touch the earth. His eyes gleam with purpose.

And riding him—

Bellerophon.

Lean and sinewed from war, a man molded by battle. His face is shadowed beneath his helmet, but a scar slashes from beneath his right eye down toward his jaw—familiar and hated. In his arms, he cradles another boulder, muscles rippling with the weight.

Penthesilea locks eyes with him.

She releases.

The arrow flies upward in a whistling arc, slicing through the air—but misses Pegasus's underbelly by the width of a hand. The horse veers smoothly, barely affected. Bellerophon's gaze sweeps downward. He sees the body among the flowers. Then he finds her.

He grins.

With casual cruelty, he releases the boulder. It drops from his grasp and plummets toward the earth. He digs his heels into Pegasus's flanks, and the beast climbs higher into the sky.

Penthesilea sprints across the clearing, drawing another arrow, then another. She fires again. Misses. Fires again. Misses still.

The sky swallows them.

Pegasus vanishes into the clouds—untouched. Victorious.

Penthesilea stares after them, her chest heaving.

Then the grief overtakes her.

She drops to her knees.

And from somewhere deep in her belly, something breaks. A cry rips from her chest—a wounded, primal sound, full of rage, sorrow, and all the things she never had time to say.

The forest listens. And mourns with her.

CHAPTER 8

The sun hovers just above the horizon, a molten disk spilling gold across the Garden of Thermodon. Between rows of myrtle and laurel trees, warriors tend their weapons—polishing, sharpening, mending what the last training session wore down. The clang of whetstone to bronze sings softly, accompanied by the rustle of wind through olive leaves.

Among them are Hippolyta and Antiope, their fingers nimble, their concentration unwavering. They speak little. Their silence is one of ease, forged by long years of battle and sisterhood.

Then—a figure stumbles into the garden.

At first, none notice. But when Penthesilea emerges fully from the tree-lined path, the sight stops breath and blade alike.

She carries a body in her arms.

The queen. Their mother.

Otrera's limbs hang limp, her hair smeared with blood and dirt, trailing like silk behind her daughter's knees. Penthesilea walks as one half-dead herself— shoulders trembling under the weight, eyes dazed. The fabric of her tunic clings to her with sweat and blood and seawater. Her strength falters.

She falls to her knees.

Gasps rise like a tide. The sharpening of blades

ceases. Several Amazons rush forward, abandoning their tasks without hesitation.

Hippolyta is the first to reach her. Antiope close behind. Together, they kneel and lift Otrera's body from Penthesilea's arms, careful not to disturb the unnatural stillness of her limbs.

"What happened?" Hippolyta breathes. Her voice is barely audible.

Penthesilea does not answer.

She stares through them—through the garden, through the moment, through the weight of time. Her fingers twitch, as though she is still holding her mother. Then, with no words and no farewell, she rises.

And walks away.

The Amazons do not stop her.

Hippolyta and Antiope remain kneeling in the dust, cradling Otrera's broken body between them. Her face, even in death, retains a dignity shaped by decades of command. The garden is still. Grief takes root in silence.

Night falls, soft as mourning cloth.

The pyre has been built in the center of the garden, beneath a fig tree heavy with fruit. Otrera lies upon it, wrapped in linen, her face exposed to the heavens. Her hands rest over her chest, a white carnation tucked between them. Twigs and dry brush surround her like a nest preparing to carry her back to the gods.

One by one, the daughters step forward.

Hippolyta. Antiope. Melanippe.

Each places a flower on her chest—a dianthus, bright and fragrant, a tribute drawn from old rites and new grief. No music plays. No prayers are spoken aloud. Only the whisper of wind through the trees and the steady beat of their hearts.

Far from the light of the torches, Penthesilea walks the shoreline, alone beneath the moon.

The sea stretches out before her, vast and silver under the stars. Waves kiss her ankles with cold foam, and she stands rooted in the sand, eyes fixed on the sky. Her face is streaked with salt—some from the sea, much from tears.

Her breath hitches.

Then she screams.

A raw, brutal sound—something torn from her soul. The scream carries out across the water, swallowed by wind, unheard by the gods.

She rips her sword from her belt and hurls it into the sea.

It vanishes with barely a splash, like it never existed at all.

She collapses to her knees, hands digging into the wet sand, fingers curling as if she could anchor herself there.

"What worth am I, if I cannot defend the ones I love?"

Her voice shakes. The sea answers with indifference.

She sees it again—clearly, as if it were unfolding before her eyes.

The forest. The moment.

Otrera crashing through the trees, voice raised in warning. The shadow above them—impossible, immense. The sound of stone shearing through branches. The queen's arms slamming into her, sending her sprawling.

Then the impact.

A boulder the size of a chariot wheel. The way her mother's body didn't move once it landed.

The flowers crushed beneath her.

White anemones.

Penthesilea's shoulders quake as she sobs, folded over her knees. The sea continues to lap at her, a tide that cannot comfort.

Then, a sound—soft, purposeful. Bare feet moving across sand.

Thyra approaches from the dark, a shawl around her shoulders. Her presence is quiet but certain, like the moonlight itself. She kneels beside Penthesilea without a word.

She reaches for her hand. Penthesilea doesn't resist.

Thyra lifts her chin gently, guiding her eyes upward.

"How can I ease your pain?"

The sobs continue, but they are softer now. Thyra wraps her arms around her, drawing her close, stroking her hair with the tenderness of someone who has known her for a lifetime.

"The death of Otrera was no fault of yours," Thyra says. "She gave her life for yours. Do not dishonor her sacrifice with despair."

"I failed her." Penthesilea's voice is cracked and low. "Where was the greatness she always spoke of?"

She looks down.

"Perhaps she was misguided in her belief."

Thyra rests her palm over Penthesilea's heart, firm but gentle.

"Your strength comes not from sword or sinew, but from here."

She waits until Penthesilea meets her eyes.

"Your mother knew of what she spoke. In time, that strength will bloom. Until then, let mine carry you."

She wipes away her tears, slow and unashamed. They sit in silence together, watching the stars reflected on the water.

The sun has risen and set again...

Fire blazes in the heart of the garden.

Drums beat in perfect synchrony, low and resonant, echoing through the Garden of Thermodon like the pulse of the earth itself. Torchlight flickers along the stone walls, casting warm firelight that dances across carvings of battles long past. The scent of oil and smoke hangs thick in the air, mingling with the delicate aroma of crushed flowers.

At the heart of the garden, the four sisters—Hippolyta, Penthesilea, Melanippe, and Antiope—form a solemn circle around the pyre. Otrera lies at its center, her body wrapped in woven linens, adorned with garlands of thyme and violet, lilies pressed into the folds of cloth like breathless prayers. Her face is calm, eternal. Still.

The drums halt.

Silence follows like a blade's edge. Every Amazon in attendance lowers to their knees, heads bowed in reverence. The stillness is complete. Not even the wind dares move.

Then the rhythm returns—louder now. Deeper. The drums erupt in a thunderous war cry, pounding like the feet of charging warriors across the ground. The garden shakes beneath the force of it.

The sisters rise. Each takes a torch, the flames hissing and leaping in their hands. In unison, they step to the four corners of the pyre and lower their torches to the linen. Fire catches quickly. A breath, a flare, and then the cloth ignites in a rush of orange and gold.

The flames climb. Fabric curls and darkens. Flower petals wither and collapse into ash, lifting into the air in glowing spirals. Sparks scatter into the sky like stars torn from their constellations. Smoke coils above them in mourning.

Tears shimmer in firelight, unhidden. They streak down cheeks, catch in lashes, glittering like falling embers. Otrera fades, her body consumed by flame. Her memory, never.

The drums quiet.

And the sky watches.

The dining hall is warm and full of noise.

Torches burn along the stone walls, casting long, flickering shadows. The great table stretches nearly the length of the hall, crowded with tribeswomen laughing, feasting, toasting. The scent of roasted meat and baked herbs rises into the beams overhead. Mugs clink together. A large candle at the center has nearly burned itself out, wax spilling over its iron base in thick rivulets.

The Amazons drink and eat in honor of their fallen queen, as tradition demands—not in sorrow, but in strength.

An Amazon warrior stands, lifting her mug above the crowd.

"To our founding queen. Though she ruled with an iron, she loved deeply with a gentleness and grace."

The hall answers as one. Mugs rise. Wine sloshes. They drink.

At the head of the table, Hippolyta stands. Regal, unshaken.

"We honor Mother by being the best of who she was. Warriors. Leaders."

Another wave of cheers. Another round of drinks.

But Penthesilea does not raise her cup. She sits in still silence, her eyes on her eldest sister. There is no celebration in her gaze—only something harder. Sharper.

"And what of the man who slain her?"

The room stills.

Hippolyta meets her sister's gaze with calm authority. "This is a time for reflection. For mourning."

"And he... just goes free."

Penthesilea rises without another word. Her movements are measured, but her rage flickers beneath the surface. She turns and exits the hall, vanishing into the corridors beyond the firelight.

The candle has melted down into a lopsided stub. The celebration endures, but its edge is softer now—muted by drink, lulled by memory. Laughter lingers, but quieter.

Penthesilea sits alone in a stone alcove, her back to the hall, her gaze turned skyward through an arched window. The stars above are unclouded and bright, scattered across the heavens in ancient order. She does not speak. She only watches.

Behind her, a soft footfall.

"Sister?"

Melanippe approaches and settles beside her. They sit shoulder to shoulder, looking up at the same star-strewn sky.

"What has captured your gaze?"

Penthesilea lifts a finger, pointing to a brilliant pinpoint of white.

"If you ever feel lost, just look to it."

Melanippe nods slowly. "Of course. The Dog Star. How could I forget?"

They sit in silence a while longer.

"You cannot go on blaming yourself," Melanippe says. "You did your best."

"It was not good enough. What is the point in being the daughter of a god if I cannot yield a bow and arrow worthy of his blood?"

Melanippe sighs with intention.

"Melanippe I–"

Melanippe cuts her off. "Do not. I was not born to battle." She locks eyes with Penthesilea, ensuring that she is heard. "But you were."

From the shadows comes another voice, looser, slurred with wine.

"I know what disrupts your aim."

Penthesilea turns. Antiope leans against a column nearby, cup in hand, eyes half-lidded but mischievous.

Melanippe frowns. "Ignore her. She is a lush."

Antiope shrugs. "Ignore me all you like. I find no difference in it."

Penthesilea's voice is quiet. "Please. Tell me."

Antiope raises her cup as if in toast. "Your bosom."

A silence falls. Penthesilea and Melanippe both glance at Penthesilea's chest.

"Antiope, you have had too much wine," Melanippe says, exasperated.

"I may be very merry," Antiope replies, lifting her chin with exaggerated dignity, "but I know what I speak of. Your bosom presses against your armor... pushes it outward. Disrupts your posture. Your aim."

Penthesilea's brow furrows. She looks down at

herself, puzzled. Not dismissive.

"Drunken nonsense," Melanippe mutters.

Antiope raises her mug in mock triumph and downs the last of her wine.

Penthesilea says nothing.

But she thinks.

Chapter 9

In the hush of late afternoon, the garden rests in the golden afterglow of the setting sun. The wind stirs gently through the high branches of a massive sacred fig tree, where a painted target cloth flutters from its thick trunk. Faded rings ripple out from a deep crimson bullseye— worn by the passage of countless arrows.

Penthesilea stands thirty paces away, eyes fixed, body taut with focus. Her bow, arrows, and bronze breastplate lie at her feet in the trampled grass. She slips the breastplate on—the metal cool against her skin—and tightens the leather straps across her back. Each movement is precise, measured, born of endless repetition. She rolls her shoulders back, plants her feet firmly, and draws in a breath.

Her fingers wrap around the bow's grip.

She nocks an arrow and raises it with slow precision. Her inhale deepens. Her exhale steadies.

She releases.

The arrow whistles through the air — and lands just off-center, veering right.

She grunts.

Another arrow. The same process. Another miss. Again, just right of the bullseye.

Frustration creeps into her brow. She tightens the straps of her breastplate, pulling them taut until the leather bites her skin.

She draws again—lets loose.

The arrow flies wide. It misses the cloth entirely and slams into a knot in the bark on the tree trunk outside the painted rings.

"Argh."

She growls in frustration. One after the other, arrows fly—some grazing the cloth's edge, some sailing off into the brush.

She throws the bow to the ground, yanks off her breastplate, and hurls it aside. It lands with a dull clatter. She drops to the grass, breath ragged, fury simmering behind her eyes.

"Here you are," a voice calls gently.

Melanippe walks into view, arms crossed, expression caught between sympathy and amusement. Her gaze drifts from the scattered arrows to the discarded gear.

"Please tell me you are not seriously entertaining the idea spewed by our lush of a sister," Melanippe says, arching a brow.

"I had to try," Penthesilea mutters, pulling herself to her feet, wincing slightly. She favors one leg as she stands, stiff from the exertion.

Melanippe sighs. "And?"

"It pains me to admit it... but she may be right."

Melanippe stares. "Surely you are not saying your aim suffers because—"

"—because of my chest," Penthesilea finishes, dryly. "The breastplate sits forward, tilting my stance."

Melanippe's face contorts. "That may be the most foolish thing—"

"It hinders my draw — my shoulders fall from their line with each attempt."

Penthesilea stoops to retrieve the loose fabric from Melanippe's helm—the one fluttering unnoticed and yanks it off.

Melanippe yelps, "What the…"

She lifts it, considering it. "I need your help."

Before Melanippe can protest, Penthesilea lifts the fabric across her chest and turns around.

"Pull it tight. As tight as you can."

Melanippe sputters. "You cannot be serious."

"Just do it."

Grumbling under her breath, Melanippe steps forward and wraps the cloth tightly around Penthesilea's chest, binding it flat. She knots it securely.

Penthesilea wastes no time. She retrieves her bow, nocks another arrow, and releases.

Thwack. Dead center.

Her eyes widen. She looks at the bullseye, stunned. Her breath catches.

Then turns to Melanippe, breathless, eyes burning with sudden clarity.

"I know what I must do."

Before Melanippe can respond, Penthesilea grabs her wrist and pulls her along.

They burst into Penthesilea's quarters. The room is

dim, lined with furs, scrolls, and a gleaming bronze mirror. Without hesitation, Penthesilea hands a sword to Melanippe.

"Hold this."

Melanippe blinks. "Why?"

Penthesilea grabs a low table, drags it forward, and lays cloths over the floor. She removes her top, kneels, and presses her chest flat against the table, arms braced.

Melanippe goes pale. "Oh no."

"You can manage this."

"No. Absolutely not."

Penthesilea retrieves a block of wood and places it between her teeth.

Melanippe stares at the sword. "Get Hippolyta. Get anyone else."

"You alone have my trust in this matter."

Silence.

Melanippe's hands tremble. "This is madness."

Penthesilea removes the wood for a moment.

"Do you know what I fear most?". She asks.

"Spiders?", Melanippe mutters.

"Hippolyta. Firstborn. Destined to be queen. Antiope... Commander of our army. And then there is me."

She exhales.

"The blood of Ares runs through all our veins, but it is my fire that must burn brightest."

She lowers her gaze to the table.

"These... An obstacle that stand before it."

Her voice catches. Then steadies.

"If I do nothing, I will fade... as though I never was."

She closes her eyes.

"Mother prayed for a daughter as formidable and courageous as our father. I will not disappoint either of them."

She meets Melanippe's eyes.

"I need you."

Melanippe hesitates. Her breath shakes. The sword feels impossibly heavy.

"Why do you always ask the impossible?"

"Because I know you can do it."

Penthesilea turns her face away and replaces the wood between her teeth.

Melanippe's hands shake.

"But... still. You ask too much of me. I cannot do this."

Penthesilea turns her head slightly and removes the wood. Her tone is cold. Precise.

"Perhaps Antiope was right."

Melanippe blinks.

"You are no warrior. No blood of Ares runs through you."

Her jaw tightens.

"Your courage has abandoned you."

Melanippe stares, unmoving.

"Not even rightfully able to hold a sword."

Her breathing shifts. Her fingers curl around the

grip. Her shoulders square.

"Raaah!"

She screams — and swings.

Thwack.

Pain sears through Penthesilea's body. Her vision goes white. Her scream is muffled by the wood. Her body crumples against the table as the blade drops to the floor.

Darkness closes in.

Chapter 10

The air in Penthesilea's sleeping quarters is thick, a slow warmth that clings to the skin and tastes faintly of lavender, herbs, and something more metallic—dried blood.

Shafts of filtered sunlight slip through narrow stone slits, their pale glow stretching in ribbons across the floor and up the cot where Penthesilea lies still. Her body is draped in clean linen, but her skin beneath is pallid, almost translucent. Only the rise and fall of her chest betrays the spark of life within her.

Her breathing is shallow—measured, fragile. The binding around her chest is layered and taut, darkened where fresh blood has seeped through. Small bowls rest in the corners of the room—filled with rainwater, wilted herbs, torn strips of linen, and the silent prayers of the woman tending her.

Thyra sits beside the cot, legs folded neatly beneath her, hands moving with gentle precision. Her brow is furrowed, not with panic, but with a steady, focused concern that comes from love seasoned by resilience. She dips a cloth into the bowl at her side, wrings it out, and presses it gently against the inflamed skin just above the bandage. Her fingers move with the delicacy of ritual—tender, practiced, and unhurried.

Penthesilea stirs. Her lips part, a soundless breath

escaping her, but her eyes remain closed.

The door creaks open.

Antiope enters, her figure framed by the glow beyond the threshold. A tray is balanced in her arms—on it, a bowl of warm broth, a wedge of barley bread, and a goblet of honeyed wine. Her leather cuirass hangs loosely around her torso, the ties unfastened, and her hair is damp with sweat.

She halts just inside the room, her sharp eyes assessing the scene.

"How is she?" she asks, voice low but not without edge.

Thyra doesn't glance up. Her hands remain busy, lifting the edge of the soaked binding with care. Beneath it, the wound is angry and raw, stitched cleanly but tight with tension. She dabs at it, the cloth red-streaked when she pulls away.

"She lost more blood than I have ever witnessed from one wound," Thyra says at last. "But she is healing quickly. Her will is stronger than her body."

Antiope exhales through her nose, stepping forward to set the tray down on a low stool. She remains standing, arms crossing over her chest.

"Only a fool maims herself chasing the illusion of greatness."

Her words are clipped, but they do not strike. Thyra's expression does not harden.

"A fool? Perhaps. But to give so much of yourself to become what you truly are... that is not foolishness. That is courage."

Antiope says nothing.

Thyra finishes rewrapping the bandage with a final pull and tuck. She smooths the linen over Penthesilea's chest, then leans down and presses a kiss to her brow—gentle, reverent. It is not the kiss of pity, but of fierce, protective love.

She gathers the bloodied cloths and herbs, the remnants of her vigil, and stands.

As she crosses the room, she passes Antiope. Their eyes meet—briefly. There is no animosity there. Only a quiet understanding between women who have each borne their own pain in silence.

"You are truly a blessing to her," Antiope says.

Thyra's smile is small but deep. "As she is to me."

She leaves with the quiet grace of someone born to shadows.

Antiope approaches the bedside, sets the tray down, and sinks to a seated position. She brushes a strand of damp hair from Penthesilea's face and gently draws her arm away from her eyes. Her gaze drops, and she lifts the sheet slightly—just enough to confirm that the tightly bound bandages remain secure across her sister's chest.

Penthesilea stirs.

Her eyelids flutter, and slowly, she wakes—eyes finding her sister's face hovering just above her.

"Here. Drink," Antiope says, lifting the bowl to her lips.

The broth is warm and savory. Penthesilea sips,

then reclines again, weary but aware. Antiope sets the bowl aside with care.

"I must be truthful," she says. "I do not believe this is something I would have done. So... bravo, sister."

She pauses, tilting her head.

"However, you needed to have only removed one."

Their eyes meet, and something dry and half-humored passes between them.

"How are you feeling?"

"The pain is no more."

"Thyra has cared for you well. She says you are healing quickly." Antiope leans back slightly. "The gift of being born of one who walks among the immortals."

Penthesilea lifts the edge of the sheet briefly and glances down at her wrapped torso. She shifts her gaze toward the window, where a soft breeze stirs the curtain of reeds.

"How long have I slept?"

"Nearly two moons."

Antiope offers her the wedge of bread.

Penthesilea shakes her head weakly. "I am without an appetite."

"You need your strength."

Reluctantly, Penthesilea takes the bread and tears a small piece. Antiope watches her, eyes thoughtful, until finally she speaks.

"What were you thinking?"

"I had to do what I felt was necessary. Now my accuracy and speed will be second to no one."

Antiope exhales, part sigh, part warning.

"I would believe you to understand, given our shared love of sport," Penthesilea says.

Antiope smiles faintly. "The passion you possess... the unyielding courage. Resolve. You are truly a daughter of Ares."

"What makes those virtues so unpleasant?"

"On the contrary. These are virtues any true warrior would be lucky to possess."

She hesitates.

"I just... I do not wish to lose a sister to darkness. This obsession will only lead to certain death."

Penthesilea meets her gaze with equal weight.

"But is that not what our destiny is as warriors?"

Antiope doesn't reply. She simply exhales and reaches for her sister's hand, pressing it once—firm and silent—before rising to her feet.

"Rest now."

She turns and leaves, her figure framed briefly in the doorway before the curtain falls shut behind her.

Left alone, Penthesilea closes her eyes.

And sleeps once more.

Chapter 11

Weeks have passed.

Themyscira's forest breathes deeply in the early morning chill. Mist snakes low across the underbrush, pooling in hollows and curling around the roots like ghostly fingers tracing forgotten trails. The canopy overhead filters the light into golden shafts that slant across the ground, catching the shimmer of dew on leaves and the gleam of something fast and thundering through the trees.

Hooves hammer the wet earth with relentless rhythm. Penthesilea rides hard, her mare galloping as if the wind itself had taken form beneath her. Their movement is a blur of unity—each command answered before it's given, each shift of weight mirrored by the animal's muscles. The forest splits before them, not out of fear, but in awe.

From the shadows, an arrow slices through the air. It lands with perfect precision in the center of a cloth target tied to a pine. The shaft quivers. Leaves settle. Silence returns.

"Ya. Ya." Her voice is firm, grounded, urging the mare forward.

Penthesilea's bow rises again, fluid as breath. She looses arrow after arrow in rapid succession, each one a syllable in the language of war. Her form is a sculpture of strength and focus, molded by years of training and unrelenting expectation. Her armor gleams with faint blue where the sun breaks through.

The forest ends.

In a rush of noise and light, she bursts from the trees onto the open shore, where sand gives way to salt-wind and sea. The horizon stretches wide and wild before her, but her focus remains grounded—fixed on the figure ahead.

A warrior steps forward, sword drawn, braced and waiting.

Without breaking stride, Penthesilea vaults from her saddle. Her body rolls smoothly into the earth, absorbing momentum, and rises with blade drawn. The warrior is already upon her. Their swords clash in a spray of sparks, the ring of bronze echoing like thunder made flesh.

High above, Hippolyta watches from a ridge. Mounted and motionless, she is an emblem of composed command—regal, unreadable. The weight of her judgment rests heavy in the air.

Below, Penthesilea falters.

The clash drives her back, foot sliding in sand. Her heel catches a rock. She stumbles, crashes to the ground. Her sword spins away—out of reach. The opponent seizes the opening, blade raised.

But Penthesilea reacts with lightning precision. She pivots, driving a brutal backward kick into her opponent's gut. The woman crashes to the ground with a gasp, weapon slipping from her hand.

They scramble. Penthesilea is faster. She reclaims her sword, rising in one fluid motion. She plants the tip at the back of the fallen warrior.

"Yield?"

The woman's breath is ragged. Pride wars with the sting of defeat. She hesitates, then lets her sword fall to the sand.

Victory flickers in Penthesilea's eyes—a hard-won fire, bright and brief.

The light in Penthesilea's sleeping quarters is soft, muted by woven drapes. She moves through the room with quiet resolve, folding a tunic, tightening leather straps, slipping polished tools into a satchel. Her focus is absolute, her pace measured.

Thyra stands nearby, arms crossed. Tension radiates from her like heat from stone.

"I will leave at first light," Penthesilea says, her voice clear and resolute.

Thyra doesn't answer right away. Her silence is filled with a storm of emotions, all warring behind her eyes.

"This is not something you should do alone," she says finally, her voice soft but heavy with fear. "At least speak with Hippolyta."

"I know my sister," Penthesilea says, not pausing in her task. "She will not be swayed. A time for reflection. A time for mourning." Her voice turns faintly bitter. "Her words at the remembrance."

Thyra suddenly crosses the room and snatches the satchel from her hands.

"I cannot let you do this."

Penthesilea looks at her. The silence between them is heavy, thick as oil. In Thyra's eyes, tears shine—but she doesn't speak.

"Why does this trouble you so?" Penthesilea asks softly.

Thyra lowers her gaze, jaw trembling.

Penthesilea's expression shifts, the hardness melting slightly. She steps closer, her voice barely above a breath.

"Ah."

She wraps her arms around Thyra, drawing her close. The satchel is forgotten between them.

"I did not know those ghosts still haunted you."

"Vengeance took my mother. My sister. I will not let it take you."

"That was long ago." Penthesilea leans back, gently cups Thyra's face. "I swear to you... I will return."

She presses a kiss to Thyra's cheek, firm and warm. Then, without hesitation, she reclaims the satchel and resumes packing. Thyra watches in silence, her sorrow quiet and unresolved.

Afternoon in the Garden of Thermodon brings a heat softened by the sea breeze. Birds chatter in the trees beyond the walls, and the scent of smoke drifts upward from a firepit ringed by carved stones.

Penthesilea crouches beside the blaze, a whetstone in hand. She draws it in steady, even passes along the curve of a battle axe—short, rounded, and heavy. The blade glows softly, catching sun and flame in its polished surface. Its handle is dark wood, scarred with use, worn smooth from war.

Across from her, a young girl—no more than ten— sits cross-legged, her eyes wide with awe. She clutches a wooden practice sword in both hands.

"You see," Penthesilea says, lifting the axe. She turns it in the light. "That is how you hone a weapon."

She hands over the whetstone. The girl nods eagerly and begins to mimic her, dragging it across the dull edge of her wooden blade with slow, serious care.

"Good."

The child beams. Her joy is silent but bright.

From across the garden, three figures approach– Hippolyta. Antiope. Melanippe. Their eyes are not smiling.

"You have always been a gifted teacher," Hippolyta says.

Penthesilea's expression hardens. She doesn't look up.

"To the girl," she says, "You are doing very well. Go show the others."

The child nods and races off, sword in hand, proud and giggling.

Penthesilea doesn't rise. She continues her work with the axe, steady as ever.

"Shall I guess..." she says, without amusement.

"She only wants to protect you," Antiope replies.

"I do not need protection from Thyra," Penthesilea says, eyes still fixed on the blade. "Nor yours."

Her fingers sift through the stones beside her, selecting a finer grit. She sets to work again, the scrape of metal filling the space between them.

"What is this you are crafting?" Melanippe asks.

"An idea."

The words are clipped, cool as the steel she sharpens.

"You are so much like Mother," Hippolyta says gently. "Resourceful. Always forging something new."

She settles onto a nearby boulder, folding her arms. "Our greatest weapons were born from such fire."

Penthesilea doesn't respond.

"It appears you have fully healed."

"I have never felt stronger."

"This is what worries us."

Penthesilea stops. She lifts her eyes at last.

"Both your pride and your arrogance," Hippolyta continues, "may well be your undoing."

"Do you not thirst for vengeance?" Penthesilea asks.

"I am with you," Antiope says, stepping forward. "But charging headlong without thought is folly. Even righteous fury must be tempered."

Penthesilea turns to Hippolyta. "I honor Mother by holding fast to her purpose. Protecting our nation."

Then to Melanippe. "And you?"

"I stand with Hippolyta."

Antiope laughs dryly. "Surely, you do not seek counsel from her?"

"Why should my voice be unworthy?" Melanippe retorts.

"You are soft. Beauty is not a shield."

"I have endured enough from you."

"Have you?"

Melanippe closes the space between them, her face fierce.

"Please do not mistake my deference to peace for weakness."

Antiope studies her, then smiles. "Well... the flower seems to have found her thorns."

"Enough," Hippolyta says sharply.

She stands, her voice firm and final.

"This is not a debate. As Queen, I forbid any pursuit of the winged horse and his rider. That is final."

Penthesilea's hand tightens around the axe handle. She rises slowly. Her eyes are fire.

"You disgrace the crown."

Hippolyta scoffs. "You would let the man who murdered Mother go unpunished. I will not."

"Mother taught us war is never waged in haste. We fight for the survival of our people. Nothing less. Anything other is futile and reckless."

"I do not view the search for vengeance as futile or harmful. It is just."

"Why must you be so stubborn?"

"Better stubborn than a coward."

"Penthesilea—" Antiope starts.

But she's already turning.

"Penthesilea," Hippolyta warns. "You are not to leave. If you defy me... do not return."

Penthesilea stops, her back to them. Her shoulders rise, pause.

Then she walks on.

Melanippe steps forward, voice soft but urgent. "Penthesilea."

"Melanippe." Hippolyta's tone is a command.

She stops, turns.

"Let her go. She is no longer of us."

Melanippe's voice is quiet. Steady.

"She will always be our sister."

She turns and vanishes into the shadows behind Penthesilea.

Hippolyta stares after them.

"Why must Penthesilea be so headstrong?"

Antiope watches the space where Melanippe disappeared.

"I am taken more by the boldness of Melanippe," she murmurs. "Perhaps there is a warrior in her yet."

Chapter 12

Penthesilea tears through the forest, breath sharp and ragged, the thrum of her heartbeat pounding like a war drum in her ears. Her limbs are on fire, each stride carved from sheer will. The quiver slaps against her back with every movement, and the bow thuds against her shoulder, forgotten in the blur of instinct and fury.

The woodland bursts open around her—branches snap, dry leaves scatter like frightened birds. Her boots crush moss, root, and fallen blossom alike as she barrels forward, a storm given form.

A sudden rustle to her right—a flash of motion. A buck—sleek, wild, untamed—erupts from the thickets. Its hooves strike the ground like thunder, its muscles coiled with the language of flight. For a brief heartbeat, they run together—girl and beast—untethered. Free. A mirror of raw power.

Without slowing, she draws an arrow, fingers moving with instinct more than thought. She notches, breathes, and looses.

It misses.

Another draw. Another shot. Bark splinters as the shaft thuds into a tree.

Miss.

She growls, baring teeth, and fires again. The arrow sails into nothing.

The buck veers into the deeper woods and vanishes into green.

Penthesilea stumbles to a halt. Her chest heaves, throat burning. Her face glistens with sweat. With a shout of frustration, she slams her palm against a tree. Bark bites into her skin as her back slides down the trunk. She sinks to the ground, shoulders slumping, defeat curdling in her chest.

"Aargh."

The cry rips from her throat and spills into the trees—raw and guttural. She curls into herself, forehead pressed to her knees, arms wrapped tightly around her shins. Her shoulders shake with quiet sobs.

The forest hushes.

Then—light.

Soft. Golden. Warming the moss-covered ground like a hearthfire. She blinks, lifting her head.

From the glow steps a figure—radiant and maternal. Ageless, yet familiar. Otrera, her mother, wrapped in something beyond silk or shadow, something divine.

"My dearest child. My joy."

Penthesilea's breath catches.

"Mother?" Her voice breaks. She squints, unable to trust her eyes. "Is it really you?"

Otrera smiles, and the warmth of it presses into Penthesilea like a balm.

"I miss you so much."

"I know your heart aches," Otrera says softly.

"I feel... like I failed you."

"You were born with the ire of your father," her mother says, stepping closer. "A storm I both feared and cherished. But one that readied you for great trials."

She kneels, her presence grounding. Solid and spectral all at once.

"I am proud of you... yet you worry me so. You must release this anger toward your sister. It is unreasoned. It will hollow you from within." Penthesilea lowers her eyes, ashamed.

"The guilt you carry... it festers. What happened was no fault of yours. Nor theirs."

"But what do I—?"

"You must forgive yourself," Otrera says, interrupting gently.

She places a hand on Penthesilea's cheek, and the younger woman leans into it, trembling.

"True strength lies not in vengeance, but release. I have seen that strength within you. Let go, and your path will rise to meet you."

Penthesilea's throat tightens. "And the man on the winged horse? I must avenge you. Our people."

"No. Let him be."

Penthesilea stiffens, surprised.

"If not for me," Otrera says, voice heavy, "he would not be orphaned. He would not have grown into a man hollowed by rage."

She pauses.

"Years of darkness shaped him. I do not wish that

path for you."

"And if I refuse?"

Otrera's hand gently lifts her daughter's chin.

"Honor is not won through violence or fury. It takes root in the display of mercy."

A long silence. Then, slowly, Penthesilea nods. It is a small gesture, but filled with weight. The fire in her eyes dims—burning not with wrath now, but reflection.

"I have accepted the fate handed down by the gods," Otrera says. "So must you. Stand alongside your sisters. Support them. Protect what I gave my life to build."

Her form begins to fade. Light seeps away, dissolving into the shadows between trees.

"No..." Penthesilea scrambles forward. "Please. I promise. Just... please do not leave me."

She is alone.

The silence hangs, broken only by the soft rustle of leaves and the distant snap of a twig.

"Penthesilea?"

She straightens quickly, swiping at her face with her forearm. Melanippe steps out from the trees, cautious, her expression concerned.

"Over here," Penthesilea says, voice hoarse.

Melanippe approaches, her steps light on the undergrowth.

"I know Hippolyta can be a bit—"

"Impossible," Penthesilea mutters.

"I was going to say controlling."

A faint smile flickers between them. The tension

loosens, if only slightly.

"But you must know she only wants what is best," Melanippe says gently. "For all that Mother built. Surely, you see that?"

Her voice quiets. "Whether you like it or not... as the daughters of Otrera, we are the compass of our nation. We must unify."

The air thickens with memory and meaning.

"I always knew there was more to you than you cared to show," Penthesilea murmurs.

Melanippe lets out a breathless laugh—half surprised, half grateful.

They walk on, side by side. Their shoulders don't touch, but their steps fall into rhythm.

As they pass, a single white anemone sways in the breeze, its pale petals stirring in the hush of the forest.

CHAPTER 13

The light in the garden room fades to a honeyed gold. Early evening settles over Themyscira like a balm, and the high stone walls of the palace glow with the warm embrace of the dying sun. Shadows lengthen across the marbled floors, stretching like quiet specters as day yields to dusk.

Inside the room, Hippolyta stands at the open window, arms loosely crossed over her chest, her gaze trained on the courtyard below. Her posture is regal, yet tinged with tension—the stance of a queen who has watched battles unfold for years, both on the field and within hearts. Her face remains composed, but her eyes are sharpened, searching, always reading between the movements of those below.

Outside, the echo of steel striking steel rings up through the stone corridors like a rallying call. In the courtyard, sparks burst where swords collide. A duel is underway—a storm of motion framed by the rhythmic clashing of blades.

Antiope, fierce and unrelenting, circles a seasoned Amazon general with the precision of a panther. Her blades flash like lightning in her hands, whistling through the air with each strike. The general meets her every blow, her own movements honed by decades of combat. Their duel is both brutal and beautiful—poetry written in muscle and reflex.

A dozen Amazons form a tight ring around them, watching intently. Their cheers rise with every deft strike and narrow dodge. They chant and stomp their feet, turning the courtyard into an arena pulsing with energy and admiration.

From the crowd's edge, another figure steps into view.

Penthesilea.

Hippolyta sees her. A flicker of warmth enters her gaze. Her lips curve, ever so slightly—one of those rare, reserved smiles saved only for her youngest sister.

Penthesilea walks with steady purpose, her boots soft against the stone. She pauses just outside the dueling ring, folding her arms as she studies the match. Her heartbeat quickens—not out of fear, but anticipation. Her fingers twitch slightly, as if yearning to grip a weapon.

Antiope lunges, sword raised in a fierce overhead arc. The general anticipates it—sidestepping with practiced ease and slamming a shoulder into her. Antiope stumbles backward and crashes to the ground, a grunt escaping as the wind is knocked from her lungs.

The crowd winces collectively.

But before defeat can settle, Antiope rolls—quick as a whip—and is on her feet in a blink. She twists into a new stance, drawing her blade back like a painter preparing a final stroke. The general presses her, but Antiope drives forward with relentless fire, forcing her opponent to retreat step by step, toward the ring's edge.

Penthesilea takes one small step forward, eyes narrowed.

"Come on, sister," she murmurs under her breath. "You can defeat her."

The clang of another strike cuts through the air. They clash again, blades singing.

But then—the general pivots sharply, plants her heel, and sweeps Antiope off her feet once more. Her sword clatters across the courtyard, skidding across the stone like a discarded crown.

Penthesilea sighs with a crooked grin. "Spoke too soon."

The general raises her blade—poised for victory.

Gasps ripple through the crowd.

But Antiope is quicker than expectation. She twists mid-fall, sweeping the general's legs out from under her with a brutal spin. As the older warrior topples, Antiope catches her falling blade in midair—turning, flipping, and driving it up until the point rests at the general's throat. Not enough to pierce, but just enough to draw a single bead of blood.

"Declare it," Antiope says, breathless but steady.

Silence.

Then, the general nods once—slow, respectful.

The courtyard erupts. Cheers burst like thunder. The Amazons flood the space with raised fists and shouts of triumph. Antiope stands, chest rising, her face split with a wild grin.

Penthesilea steps forward, her voice light with

teasing admiration.

"Congratulations, General," she calls. "Enjoy it while you can, Sister."

Antiope laughs, wiping sweat from her brow. As she passes, she ruffles Penthesilea's hair in a quick, affectionate swipe.

"What? Worry about a pretty thing like you? Never."

"Ha. Ha."

Antiope saunters away, victorious, reveling in the moment—but before she disappears into the archway, she turns over her shoulder.

"Your smile is a welcome sight." She continues onward.

Penthesilea looks up.

At the window above, Hippolyta still watches. They lock eyes—sister to sister, queen to kin.

The warmth in Hippolyta's face remains.

But for Penthesilea, the smile slowly fades. She lowers her gaze.

And walks away.

Chapter 14

Themyscira sleeps beneath a canopy of stars, her cliffs jutting like the jaws of Titans into the sea. Atop one such precipice, Penthesilea dismounts with silent reverence. The moon, full and argent, casts its silver sheen across the restless ocean, painting a glowing path that leads into the unknown.

She walks to the cliff's edge, where salt air tangles with her hair. The sea whispers below, ancient and unending. She lowers herself onto the cool grass, crossing her arms over her knees. Her gaze lifts to the stars, where constellations etched into eternity blink softly down. For a rare moment, the burdens of war and title fall away.

But stillness rarely lasts.

A distant sound — grating, foreign — breaks the night. Penthesilea straightens. Her breath catches.

Far below, a war galley splits the tide. Its bronze prow gleams like a blade in moonlight. It crashes into the shore with violent finality, its hull creaking, anchoring in the sand like a challenge cast in steel.

Figures spill from its belly — soldiers in polished armor, their movements rigid, practiced. At their head: Heracles. Giant of myth, son of Zeus, a walking tempest in lion's skin and iron.

Another figure flanks him. Younger. Slimmer. Yet no less proud. Theseus, prince of Athens, helmet shining, eyes sharp. At his side trots a Laconian hound, alert and bound by silent command.

Across the beach, movement stirs in the trees.

From the shadow of palms emerge Hippolyta and Antiope — luminous and unflinching, firelight incarnate. Behind them, forty Amazons fan out like a living tide of steel and precision.

The air thickens.

The leaders step forward. Heracles' gaze is drawn to the belt at Hippolyta's hip — the girdle of Ares, glowing softly beneath her cloak.

"No need for alarm," Heracles calls, his voice a low thunder. "We mean no harm."

Hippolyta lifts her chin. "And you are?"

"Heracles. Son of Zeus. This is Theseus."

She studies him with quiet disdain. "And what business have you here?"

"We seek rest. Our voyage has been long."

"This is not a good time for us to entertain visitors. I suggest you be on your way."

Theseus lets his gaze linger on the gathered Amazons, bold in his curiosity. His eyes find Antiope — equal parts grace and menace in every controlled breath.

"Are the stories true?" he asks. "Are the Amazons merciless toward men?"

Antiope's tone is edged steel.

"That is not something you wish to test."

Yet Theseus steps closer, until they stand toe to toe. A heartbeat from confrontation.

"To fall by your blade would be the most honorable fate I could meet."

Antiope tenses. Their gazes clash like flint and steel.

Hippolyta mutters dryly,

"A real charmer."

Above them, unseen, Penthesilea crests the ridge. Her eyes sweep the beach below, brows knitting.

"What the…"

On the sand, Antiope shoves Theseus back. Her stance says everything words cannot.

Theseus stiffens, teeth clenched.

Heracles offers a strained smile.

"To Antiope — disregard my good friend. His tongue works faster than his mind."

Theseus grins, but it's hollow.

Heracles turns back to Hippolyta.

"Forgive us. We will seek a place further along the coast. We desire not to trouble you."

A curt nod from Hippolyta ends the encounter — or seems to.

Heracles casts a glance to Theseus, then subtly gestures to his men — a slight tilt of the head. To the shoreline. Quiet. Calculated.

High above, Penthesilea crouches, her form still as stone. A sentinel. Her sisters turn their backs to the Greek men who claimed civility. Heracles. Theseus. Liars dressed in bronze. She watches.

The moon is high and pitiless, bathing the beach in

silver light. From her perch at the cliff's edge, the scene below looks almost serene. But instinct coils in her stomach. Her gaze narrows.

The air shifts.

Penthesilea sees it—Heracles' subtle nod to Theseus.

Her breath stills.

Theseus lifts his hand, fingers flicking lazily toward the dog at his side.

The Laconian explodes forward.

The world narrows. Time fractures. Sound dulls to a heartbeat.

The beast tears across the sand, muscles rippling, eyes locked on Hippolyta.

Penthesilea's voice shreds the silence.

"No."

Time snaps back. Her breath returns in a gasp.

Below, Hippolyta whirls. The dog leaps, fangs glinting. Her arms rise just in time to catch it mid-air. The force nearly topples her, but she holds. Snarling, she hurls the beast down the beach in a furious arc, its body slamming into the sand, unmoving.

Heracles reacts first. His head jerks toward the cliffs, eyes locking on Penthesilea just before she vanishes into the brush.

She's already moving.

She runs like death is chasing her.

Branches whip her skin. Her lungs burn. Rocks bite into her feet. The wind roars in her ears, but all she hears is the rising chaos below. Her sisters are down there. And it has begun.

The beach erupts. Screams pierce the air. The clash of steel strikes like thunder. Amazons charge into the Greek line, blades drawn, shields up, war cries echoing off the stone walls behind them.

Still flat on his back, Heracles grabs Hippolyta by the legs and throws her aside with monstrous strength. She hits the ground hard, rolls, and rises with blood on her lip.

She lunges—only for his fist to catch her mid-strike. They both crash into the sand, wind knocked from them. Her sword is lost, spinning end over end into the dark.

Antiope duels Theseus nearby. Their blades whisper and clash, too graceful for a battlefield. They circle like dancers at the edge of something deadly. Their faces show more curiosity than hatred.

Heracles rises again, gritting his teeth. Blood drips from a gash across his brow.

He charges.

Hippolyta braces. At the last instant, she drives her palm into his chest. The blow sends him skidding backward, dust and sand billowing around him.

She turns, searching for her weapon.

But he recovers faster. He crashes into her again, lifting her off her feet and slamming her into the beach. She hits with a brutal crunch, groaning. The belt slips free from her hip and lands yards away in the sand.

They rise together.

They collide.

This time, Hippolyta doesn't yield. Her muscles lock against his. Heracles falters, blinking from the impact, disbelief crossing his face.

And then—

Penthesilea bursts from the tree line.

A scream tears from her throat, a raw chord of fury. Her sword flashes in one hand, a battle axe gleams in the other. She carves through Greek soldiers like they're woven from straw. Blood sprays. Bones snap beneath her blade.

"Hippolyta! Antiope!"

She sees them—Hippolyta down, Antiope entangled with Theseus.

Their swords flirt with flesh but pull back every time. A game. A dare.

Heracles lifts Hippolyta once more and slams her to the ground like she weighs nothing. She gasps, crawling now, reaching—

The belt.

He sees it too. He reaches for his sword.

Penthesilea reacts without thought.

She drops her blade. The axe sinks into a Greek soldier's spine as she draws her bow. Breath in. Fingers pull.

The arrow screams.

It strikes Heracles in the chest—just off the heart. The impact stuns him, makes him stagger. His hand flies to the wound, blood already darkening the leather.

Hippolyta twists onto her side, eyes catching his

pain.

Heracles snarls. He rips the arrow free and locks eyes with Penthesilea. There is no recognition. Only rage.

She draws again.

He raises a hand.

The second arrow is caught in flight, just inches from his cheek.

They stare across the battlefield—hunter and prey, but it is unclear which is which.

She tosses the bow and runs.

Heracles kicks Hippolyta aside and lunges for the belt. His hand closes over it. With a roar that splits the night, he calls for retreat.

On the shoreline, Theseus hears it.

He hesitates—his blade pressed to Antiope's shoulder.

Then he throws her over his back and runs.

She doesn't resist.

Penthesilea reaches Hippolyta, who coughs, blood bubbling at the corner of her mouth. Her armor is dented, her body trembling.

"Hippolyta. Have you been harmed?"

Penthesilea kneels beside her, scanning for wounds. Hippolyta lifts her head with a small, defiant smile. "He suffered more by my hand than I by his. You might pity him, were he not a foe."

Penthesilea helps her sit up, bracing her gently.

"Now is not the time for jest."

"Speaking of jest..." Hippolyta looks around.

"Where is Antiope?"

Penthesilea scans the battlefield—then she sees it.

A trireme, gliding from the bay.

Theseus aboard.

Antiope slung over his shoulder like spoils.

"Antiope."

Penthesilea reaches for her bow—nothing.

Her gaze sweeps the beach.

Hippolyta's sword lies half-buried in the sand. She runs to it, fingers closing around the hilt.

But the ship is already too far.

She turns.

The beach is a graveyard.

Smoke wafts from the scorched dunes. Bodies lie tangled—Amazon and Greek alike. The wind carries the scent of iron and ash.

A groan rises nearby.

A Greek soldier, half-buried in a broken shield, reaches for something in the sand. His face is smeared with blood, his breath shallow.

Penthesilea stomps over.

She grabs him by the chest plate and drags him, armor scraping and clattering against the ground, each step pulling him closer to judgment.

The tide pulls in behind her. The war has begun.

And she will not stop.

CHAPTER 15

The garden is no longer a place of serenity.

Moonlight filters through the olive trees, washing the stone paths in silver. Flower petals flutter in the breeze, ghostly and silent—indifferent witnesses to the violence now rooted in their soil.

Penthesilea stands over the kneeling Greek, a towering silhouette of fury, lit by torchlight and purpose. He is broken—his armor torn, face streaked with blood, lips trembling. His hands are bound behind his back, the rope dark with his own sweat.

His eyes dart upward, locking on hers. She stares down without a flicker of pity.

"You have but two more chances to share the plans of Heracles," she says, her voice calm. Too calm.

The man says nothing.

She tilts her head and kneels, slowly, almost gently —bringing herself level with his face. Then she grabs his jaw with one hand, forcing it open as if inspecting livestock. With the other, she presses the edge of her blade to his tongue.

And drives it through.

His scream is strangled. The sound gurgles from his throat, thick and wet, expressing a concession–*Okay. I'll tell you.*

She removes her blade.

He gasps, blood seeping over his chin. Still panting, still alive.

"He is to take the belt to King Eurystheus of Tiryns," he stammers, voice shredded from pain. "Pausing in Troy along the way."

Penthesilea's eyes narrow. The information settles into her bones like ice.

She smiles.

"See?" she says softly, like a mother indulging a child. "As easy as a child at play."

She slices the ropes with one clean stroke. The man's arms drop, shaking.

"Go," she says, rising to her feet.

He hesitates. A flicker of hope glows behind the terror in his eyes. He scrambles upright, wobbling, blood dripping from his mouth, and turns to flee.

Penthesilea watches him go. Her expression doesn't change.

She lifts her bow.

An arrow slips into place.

She whistles—sharp, piercing.

The Greek turns back at the sound.

The arrow hits him before his eyes can widen. A perfect shot, the shaft buried deep through the center of his skull. His body stiffens, then folds backward into the grass.

Penthesilea lowers the bow, not even watching him fall.

She turns. Walks away.

The blood-streaked garden returns to silence

behind her, as if nothing had happened at all.

A soft breeze stirs the curtains in Hippolyta's quarters. Oil lamps flicker in the stone recesses, casting a golden warmth over the cool gray walls. She lies on a low bed, her armor removed, a fresh bandage wrapping her ribs. Bruises bloom purple and black beneath her collarbone.

The door opens with a whisper. Penthesilea enters, a ghost of the garden's shadows still clinging to her.

"How are you feeling?" she asks.

Hippolyta shifts, breath hitching faintly at the movement.

"I have suffered worse in our own battles."

They share a dry chuckle — warriors' laughter, sharpened by memory.

Penthesilea sits beside her. Close, but not intrusive.

"I thought you left in search of the winged horse and its rider," Hippolyta says, studying her sister's face.

"Let us say my mind and heart no longer walk the same path as before."

"A fortunate shift for us."

"Heracles is gone. I came to see how you were faring before I leave to reclaim Antiope and your belt."

"Leave the belt. It is not worth the blood it would cost. But Antiope..."

She pushes the sheet aside and sits up, jaw set against pain.

Penthesilea rises, already bracing for the argument.

"Your wounds are still fresh."

"You shall not go without me."

"That is unwise. Stay here. Heal properly."

Hippolyta plants her feet on the floor, slow but unyielding.

"Have you forgotten? I, too, am born of Ares. My wounds shall mend as we journey on."

Penthesilea watches her — truly watches her — torn between loyalty and fear.

"Is this you speaking as my queen or my sister?"

Hippolyta holds her gaze. "Is one different from the other?"

A long silence hangs between them. Heavy. Unspoken truths caught in its weight.

Penthesilea exhales.

"So be it. I shall ready the horses."

She turns and exits, her footsteps lost in the hush of stone.

Hippolyta remains still for a moment, bracing herself with a hand on the wall. She straightens, every movement a careful betrayal of pain — and pride. She hides the wince behind clenched teeth.

CHAPTER 16

The forest breathes in the dark — a slow, pulsing life of cricketsong and distant wings. Under the canopy, the world glows silver and black. Leaves shimmer faintly with dew, and somewhere far off, an owl calls once, then falls silent.

Penthesilea rides at a steady pace, her silhouette tall in the saddle, spear resting beside her thigh, bow and quiver slung across her back. Beside her, Hippolyta moves more rigidly. Each jolt of the horse sends pain flashing through her, though she hides it well. Almost.

Almost.

Penthesilea notices. She murmurs to her mount.

"Whoa."

Her gaze shifts to her sister. "We will rest our heads here."

But Hippolyta urges her steed forward, a defiant flick of the reins.

"No. We are too far behind. We must press on."

Penthesilea catches up in two strides, reaching out — firm fingers seize Hippolyta's reins. The horses snort and paw at the earth, restless.

"Exile me if you must," she says, voice hard but low. "But we rest here."

They halt. The trees creak overhead in the breeze, their leaves whispering ancient warnings. For a moment, only the breath of the forest moves between them.

"We will find them," Penthesilea says. "I swear it."

Hippolyta hesitates, then nods.

They dismount in silence, the soft rustle of leather and armor lost in the murmuring dark.

Smoke coils upward, thin and blue against the night. A fire crackles between the sisters, warming a circle of moss and earth. Half a wild hare roasts on a spit fashioned from ashwood and twine. Its scent mingles with pine and distant myrrh.

They sit across from one another — no longer in the saddle, no longer warriors for this breath of time, just two daughters of Ares under the stars.

Hippolyta stares into the flames, her shoulders relaxed but her eyes heavy.

"Peace dwells here," she murmurs. "The night sounds. The gentle breeze."

Penthesilea tears into the meat, grease on her fingers, silent in her reply.

"You will die as ornery as a boar," Hippolyta quips.

"And you will not?"

A faint smirk trades hands between them. Small, genuine. A soft thing in the hardness of the world.

Hippolyta tilts her chin upward. The sky sprawls, vast and glittering. A single star gleams brighter than the rest — ancient, unmoving.

"Do you believe Mother is watching?"

Penthesilea doesn't hesitate. "Always."

They sit quietly, faces lit gold by firelight, bodies wrapped in the hush of the trees and the pulse of memory. The flames snap. Somewhere above, a branch creaks.

They look at each other.

Then, a short laugh — more exhale than sound — escapes Hippolyta. She shifts, gathering her thoughts like one preparing for battle.

"Thank you."

Penthesilea glances sideways, wary of the softness in her sister's tone.

"If it were not for you I—"

"Hippolyta, you owe me no—"

"Let me speak. Please?"

Penthesilea stops.

"You and I..." Hippolyta begins, her voice steady but hushed. "There has always been a distance between us. Distance I regret. Yet... I allow it to grow."

A silence. Then, slowly, her voice again:

"You are my sister. I have loved and respected you as such. Though I have failed to say so."

Penthesilea's throat tightens.

"And I, you."

But Hippolyta lifts her hand — a quiet command.

"Mortality brings clarity."

She gazes into the fire.

"I have ruled as best I could... being a guide to you and Melanippe in the absence of our mother."

Her eyes meet Penthesilea's. The warmth there is unguarded, rare. A fire not of fury, but of belonging.

"You must know... My sisters mean more to me than anything. If I have ever made you feel slighted, I am sorry."

Penthesilea blinks once. Tears burn at the edges of her vision. She leans forward and draws Hippolyta into her arms.

The embrace is fierce and quiet.

For a long time, neither moves.

When they pull back, it is gently. They wipe at their eyes, neither ashamed of the tears that have traced their cheeks.

"We should rest," Penthesilea says, her voice soft again.

Hippolyta nods and lies down, wrapping her cloak around her shoulders. She exhales as though releasing more than breath.

Penthesilea joins her on the soft grass, one eye still on the dark edges of the trees.

Above them, Sirius — the Dog Star — glimmers like a sentinel.

CHAPTER 17

The sun hangs high above Troy, casting its ancient stones in molten gold. Heat shimmers along the battlements, and the wind carries with it the scent of olive oil, sweat, and salt from the distant sea.

Penthesilea and Hippolyta ride side by side through the haze. Dust curls beneath their horses' hooves as they approach the city gates—towering slabs of carved limestone, proud and unyielding. Atop the battlements, sentries lean forward. Spears shift in wary hands.

Then, a shout. A wave.

The gates creak open.

The sisters pass beneath the archway and into the pulsing heart of the city.

The Agora bursts with life. A swirl of motion and sound. Vendors shout over one another, waving bolts of dyed linen, strings of dried figs, and polished bronze rings. The air is rich with roasting meat and sandal-leather. Doves scatter at ankle-height. A child weaves between stall legs, laughing.

Penthesilea and Hippolyta ride slowly through the square, scanning faces.

A shimmer of silk catches Hippolyta's eye. Soft green fabric, caught in the wind like water in motion. She slows, drawn to it. Without a word, she drifts toward the chiton display, dismounting almost absently.

Penthesilea doesn't notice right away. Then, frowning, she turns.

Just beside the fabric, silent and unnoticed, a young man fingers a basket of copper trinkets. His face is smooth but alert. He turns and slips into the crowd without a sound.

Hector.

Penthesilea's gaze cuts across the market. Her body tenses. Something has shifted in the air.

"Hippolyta."

Hippolyta glances back.

Penthesilea's eyes fix on a figure slipping between booths. A man in a bronze helmet. Familiar in every motion.

"Hippolyta! "

Hector glances back from across the square. His eyes meet Penthesilea's—then flick to Hippolyta. A flicker of recognition crosses his face. Concern. He moves toward her, quickening his pace.

But before he can reach her, she drops a bracelet from her hand.

Penthesilea's voice cuts through the din. "Come on!"

She grabs Hippolyta by the arm and pulls her away, weaving through the crowd. Her steps are swift. Purposeful.

Behind them, Hector follows.

"What has taken over you?" Hippolyta demands,

breath short as they dodge a man carrying amphorae.

"There," Penthesilea points. "In the red chiton."

Hippolyta squints. Then—

"Theseus?"

"Theseus."

He turns.

Their eyes lock.

For a heartbeat, the market seems to hold its breath.

Then his hand shifts, inching toward his hip.

He bolts.

Penthesilea lunges forward, breaking into a run. Hippolyta follows. Behind them, Hector veers off, taking a separate path around the market's edge.

The alleys of Troy wind like veins, narrow and cluttered with baskets, crates, and drying laundry. Theseus slips between them like smoke, footsteps silent against stone. Penthesilea is gaining—each stride closing the distance.

He rounds a corner sharply.

A door slams open.

He slips inside.

Penthesilea barrels through the same door moments later, sword already drawn.

The light dims. The air thickens. The inn smells of sour wine and old sweat.

A sound behind her. A breath, out of place.

She pivots.

Blades crash. Sparks leap from the contact. Theseus stands before her, weapon raised, teeth bared in a half-smile.

They circle.

His footwork is nimble. Measured. Hers is silent, precise. She watches his eyes more than his hands.

Then he shoves her, trying to break the rhythm. She doesn't budge. Her counter is swift—a forward lunge. He twists. Dodges.

He charges.

She sidesteps—fluid as water—and knocks the blade from his hand. It clatters to the floor.

A kick to his chest sends him crashing onto his back. Dust swirls. He groans, dazed, but already pushing up to his knees.

Penthesilea plants her boot near his arm, sword poised above him.

"Where is she?"

He breathes hard, eyes darting.

Silence.

She steps forward, blade pressing against the crook of his arm.

"Speak, or I will take you apart, piece by piece. And nothing would bring me more pleasure than to see your blood warm my blade."

He laughs—dry and contemptuous.

"You Amazons. This famed lust for blood... Do you not find it just a touch theatrical?" He tilts his head. "Pageantry without purpose, if you ask me."

Outside, Hector watches from a window, his eyes wide with disbelief. He turns and vanishes.

Inside, Theseus shifts subtly.

His eyes dart to the fallen sword. A twitch of his heel. A coiled spring.

He lunges for it.

Penthesilea moves instantly—sword raised to strike—but her blade meets another.

The clang resounds through the stone walls.

She recoils, startled.

Another figure stands between them now, poised and unreadable.

Antiope.

"Theseus," she says, calm. "Well timed, beloved."

Penthesilea stares, jaw tight with disbelief.

Behind her, Hippolyta stumbles into the room, clutching her side.

The quarters are small but clean, washed in light from the high window. The scent of fresh thyme lingers. Antiope leads them inside.

Theseus lounges with casual confidence. Hippolyta moves stiffly. Penthesilea enters last, eyes flicking between them. A small flower is braided into Antiope's hair.

"What brings you here?" Antiope asks, her voice light.

Penthesilea and Hippolyta exchange glances—confusion plain on their faces.

"We came for you," Penthesilea says. "I saw him carry you away to his ship."

"You know well I need no saving."

"And still, you stayed by his side."

"Theseus," the man says, waving with a grin. "Right here. Not a shade nor a ghost."

Penthesilea narrows her eyes at him. He winks.

Antiope turns to him with a look almost tender.

"What can I say? My heart has grown fond of him."

She turns back to her sisters.

"Tomorrow, we leave for Athens. We are to marry."

"Fond of him? Married?" Penthesilea steps forward, her voice fraying. "Antiope... what has become of you?"

She reaches to touch her sister's head, fingers gently combing the hair as if to find injury beneath the surface.

"Did he strike you? Rattle your wits somehow? And this flower dangling from your hair?"

Antiope brushes her hand away with a faint smile.

"I am unharmed."

She glances at Theseus again.

"What can I say? He has captured my heart."

She pauses.

"He is my family now."

"And what of us?" Penthesilea's voice lowers. "Your sisters?"

"I love you both. But I do not wish to return to Themyscira."

"Theseus," Hippolyta mutters, studying him, "he is rather... alluring."

He spreads his arms, amused. "Am I not?"

Penthesilea shakes her head slowly, the expression on her face equal parts sorrow and disdain.

CHAPTER 18

The air inside the king's chamber feels carved from stone and silence. Torches hiss in their sconces, casting long shadows that stretch like fingers across the marble floor.

Paris stands beside his father, arms crossed, brow drawn. Paleos, the ever-stoic advisor, speaks with the calm of a man bearing a dagger in his hands.

"Achilles?" King Priam asks, his voice thinned by disbelief. "The Achilles? Are you certain?"

Paleos gives a short, solemn nod. "Yes, my king. The message was clear. Achilles has joined Menelaus in his campaign against Troy."

The name sinks into the room like a stone into deep water.

"Oh, dear," Priam breathes, and something in him buckles. He turns from the others, one hand bracing the wall, as though his body cannot carry the weight of the name. Achilles. That name carries storms.

Then — the door creaks open.

Hector enters, posture straight, senses sharpened by the heaviness that clings to the air like smoke.

"What is this?" he asks, already wary.

King Priam does not turn. "Paleos brings word… Achilles stands with Menelaus."

Dread takes a hold of King Priam.

"What are we to do now?"

Paris steps forward, ever the tactician, his tone measured. "Certainly, one man cannot tip the scales of battle."

Hector looks at his brother — not dismissively, but with a quiet pity.

"Brother, Achilles is no mere man."

He lets the truth linger, then speaks again, slower.

"His strength is unmatched… and his skills are legendary."

Paris draws a breath, searching for a foothold in the dark. "No one is without flaw. He must possess a weakness."

Hector's eyes turn inward for a moment. A memory. A whispered tale.

"His heel," he says. "That is his weakness."

A silence follows.

"But… to strike there would require perfection in battle."

King Priam closes his eyes. "We had a fighting chance against Menelaus and Agamemnon. But Achilles…"

He shakes his head.

"I fear we cannot withstand him."

But Hector's voice shifts — not defiant, but steady. Steeled.

"Our fate may have changed, but not as we fear."

All eyes fix on him.

King Priam straightens, the fatigue in his body

briefly forgotten.

Hector's gaze sharpens. "Only just now, I saw an Amazon sparring with Theseus."

"The Amazons?" Priam's voice lifts in disbelief. "Here? In Troy?"

"Yes, Father," Hector confirms. "It has been some time since I last visited Themyscira. I wish to invite them to dinner… that we may persuade them to reconsider."

Paris looks unconvinced. "Do you truly believe that to be possible?"

But King Priam says nothing. He studies Hector a moment longer.

"We must try," Hector says quietly.

The Agora still hums with life, though the heat of the day has begun to soften. Penthesilea and Hippolyta walk side by side once more, but their strides carry the tension of all they've seen — and heard.

"That was most unexpected," Hippolyta says, her voice low and musing. "Given how she has always recoiled at the very thought of coupling."

Penthesilea scowls slightly. "His swordplay reveals more pride than precision."

Hippolyta raises a brow. "Perhaps he wields other weapons with greater… confidence."

Penthesilea grimaces as though she'd swallowed rot. "The thought alone curdles my spirit."

"Come now, sister. Where is your sense of humor?"

Before Penthesilea can reply, a figure steps into

their path.

Tall. Familiar.

Swords slide from their scabbards before the man can even open his mouth.

He holds up his hands. "Do you not remember me?"

Penthesilea narrows her gaze, eyes raking over his face. Her grip tightens on the hilt, unsure.

"You came to Themyscira," she says slowly. "Long ago."

He nods. "You were but girls then… playing in the garden."

He turns toward the queen. "Hippolyta, is it not?"

She lowers her sword an inch, warily.

"And you… Penthesilea. I remember you well."

The tension begins to ease, their hands retreating from their weapons — but their bodies remain rigid.

"You ought to show greater care in how you come upon others," Hippolyta says.

The man smiles, but not mockingly.

Penthesilea watches him closely. "Why do you smile?"

"Forgive me. Never did I expect to see you here, within these city walls."

She turns, curt. "Hippolyta. Come."

But the man steps quickly into their path, not threatening — only earnest.

"Wait. Please."

A pause.

"Would you consider dining with me and my family tonight?"

CHAPTER 19

Troy's allied township of Lyrnessus burns beneath a sky smothered in smoke.

Dusk bleeds across the heavens in streaks of rust and indigo, as oil lamps flicker weakly in the growing dark — their flames struggling to compete with the greater fire consuming the town. Narrow streets twist through the wreckage, where once-proud oikos now lean drunkenly or lie in heaps of shattered timber. Roofs collapse under their own weight. Clay walls crumble inward, exposing blackened hearths and the skeletal remains of family tables.

The scent is everywhere — scorched olive oil, charred meat, the coppery tang of blood thick on the tongue. And over all of it: smoke, cloying and endless, coiling up to the darkening sky like a prayer the gods will not hear.

Bodies lie twisted across the dirt paths, some still smoldering, others already stiffening, hands curled as if still reaching for someone who never came.

Achilles steps from the threshold of a burning house.

The flames behind him crackle and spit. He doesn't look back.

He bites into an apple — slow, casual — its crisp crunch an eerie punctuation against the backdrop of screams. His gaze drifts across the destruction like a connoisseur at a banquet. His men spread through the town like a sickness, kicking in doors, dragging out survivors, torching whatever still stands.

To Achilles, it is routine. The pace of conquest. The rhythm of war.

Then movement — slight, but sharp — catches his eye.

A boy, no older than ten, darts from the shadows of a collapsed wall. Dust and ash coat his face, but his eyes are wide, white with terror. He halts when he sees Achilles.

Their eyes lock.

Time seems to narrow.

Then the boy runs.

Achilles grins.

Another bite of apple.

Behind him, a struggle breaks the air.

"Unhand me," a voice commands — not shrill, not pleading, but fierce.

He turns.

Patroclus approaches, dragging a young woman through the debris. She is bloodied but unbowed, strands of black hair falling loose around a face too proud for fear. Her clothing is torn, but her spine remains unbroken.

"She was hiding," Patroclus says. "Declares she is the wife of Mynes. I thought you would prefer to deal with her yourself."

Achilles tosses his apple core to the dirt.

"You know me well, Patroclus."

They stop a few paces apart. The woman wrenches free from Patroclus' grasp with a sudden twist of strength, stepping forward to stand alone.

She faces Achilles head-on.

"Release me, you murderous brute."

Her voice cuts cleanly through the smoke.

Achilles studies her, head tilted. A slow smile curls his lips.

"Beautiful and fiery."

His words hang.

"What is your name?"

"I am Briseis, wife of King Mynes."

She speaks the title with pride, even now, as the town turns to ash around her. Her breath comes quick, but her eyes never waver.

"What has Lyrnessus done to you? What is our crime?"

"Being an ally of Troy is crime enough."

Briseis blinks once — the first crack in her composure. But she recovers fast, clenching her fists at her sides.

"If you will not release me… kill me."

Her chin lifts.

"You have taken my husband and all that I held dear."

Achilles steps closer, and the firelight carves deep shadows into his features.

"Would it ease your soul to know that your king

died fighting bravely?"

The answer, for a flicker of a moment, threatens to reach her. Then fury hardens her again.

Achilles shrugs, as though she's a wager he has no need to win.

"Tie her up. Strap her to a horse. I will take her as a prize."

Patroclus hesitates. "Achilles. Are you certain?"

Achilles glances at him — slow, sharp.

He takes another bite of his apple.

"Would that be a problem for you?"

Patroclus exhales through his nose, then grabs Briseis' arm. She struggles, teeth bared, but he drags her away with practiced ease.

Behind them, Achilles watches. The apple crunches again between his teeth as the town burns around him — a war god walking through the ruin, smirking at the flames.

CHAPTER 20

Laughter ripples through the high chamber like echoes from a warmer time.

Golden torchlight dances along the carved walls, flickering against tapestries that depict gods and battles, triumphs and tragedies. A long banquet table stretches beneath the vaulted ceiling, weighed down by the remains of an opulent meal — half-eaten figs, bones stripped of meat, goblets toppled on their sides. The air is rich with the scent of wine, roasted lamb, and the slow burn of spiced incense curling from bronze braziers in each corner.

At the table, a gathering of power and beauty.

King Priam, silver-haired and sharp-eyed despite the years. Queen Hecuba, dignified, her bearing regal even in repose. Beside them: Hector and his wife, Andromache — young, composed, wise beyond her years. Paris lounges near Helen, whose presence is as effortless as it is incendiary. Across from them, Penthesilea and Hippolyta sit with posture forged by a life in armor.

The laughter dies gently, giving way to a silence that is not empty but content.

"I could tell a hundred more stories about my sons…" King Priam says, a hand raised mid-gesture.

"Please, love," Hecuba interrupts gently. "I suspect they have endured quite enough."

"I agree, Mother," Hector says with a faint smirk.

His eyes meet Penthesilea's across the table. For a fleeting moment, something like amusement flickers between them. Her smile is small, contained — a blade's edge hidden beneath silk.

But Hippolyta leans forward now, gaze direct.

"Forgive my bluntness," she says, "but why were we invited here?"

The mood shifts. King Priam glances to Hecuba, who rises with the grace of a practiced queen. Her hands are clasped lightly at her waist.

"Shall I?"

"Please, my dear," Priam says, his voice softening.

Hecuba gives a subtle nod, and at once, the tempo of the room begins to change. Helen and Andromache both stand, glancing to their husbands.

"It was a pleasure meeting you both," Andromache offers with sincerity.

Penthesilea inclines her head. "Andromache... The pleasure was truly ours."

Hector leans to kiss his wife, and Penthesilea watches — silent, unreadable.

Helen's voice is honeyed. "May we be graced by your company again soon."

"Good night," Hippolyta replies with quiet formality.

Paris kisses Helen's hand, more show than sentiment. Then the women are gone, their silks whispering across marble as they retreat into the shadows.

A stillness settles over the remaining few.

Priam and Hector share a glance — brief, but loaded with unspoken strategy.

The king turns toward the Amazons. "Your presence has given us hope... Perhaps your mother would reconsider aiding in our defense.

Unknowingly. "How does she fare?"

Hippolyta lowers her gaze. "She passed... not long ago."

Penthesilea's voice follows, hard and precise.

"She was murdered."

Hippolyta shoots her a warning look — but says nothing more.

"You have my deepest condolences," King Priam says solemnly.

"And mine," Hector adds. He turns toward Hippolyta, eyes steady. "Then... you are queen now."

"I am," she answers. Her tone holds the weight of it.

"You said reconsider aid?" she prompts.

Priam exhales. "Troy is under siege by the Greeks."

He pauses, the words sitting heavy in the air.

"Our army stands strong... enough, I believe, to face Menelaus and Agamemnon. But..."

Another pause.

"Achilles has joined them."

The name lands like a falling sword.

Smoke without fire. A pressure in the chest.

"Under siege?" Hippolyta asks, brow furrowed. "We have seen no signs of—"

"The battle is along the shore," Paris interjects, voice sharper than expected. "But it will reach our gates before long."

"In the meantime," Hector says, "they assail our allies."

Penthesilea leans forward slightly. "And this Achilles? Do you fear him?"

Hector does not flinch. "Even the boldest fear him." "They say he fights like a lion unleashed. Merciless. Swift. Unstoppable."

"Then he has yet to meet his match," Penthesilea replies without hesitation.

Her eyes lock onto Hector's. A spark passes between them. Hippolyta notices.

"What provoked the Greeks to such fury?" she asks, cutting the moment clean.

Hector looks to Paris, who straightens, reluctant.

"Helen," he says.

Penthesilea narrows her gaze. "What of her?"

"She is the wife of Menelaus," Paris replies.

"And yet," Hippolyta says coolly, "she is here as your lover?"

"Menelaus invited us to Sparta," Paris explains, "seeking friendship between our kingdoms. But there… Helen and I…"

He hesitates. "We fell in love. I asked her to return with me."

"You stole his wife?" Hippolyta's tone is flat, cold.

"She came of her own will."

Hector gives a small, almost imperceptible nod —
as though validating his brother, if only in part.

The Amazons say nothing.

"And thus," Priam says, "Menelaus called upon his
brother. Together, they vowed to bring ruin upon Troy."

He gestures to them.

"Hector saw you in the square and dared to
hope..."

Hippolyta's answer is immediate. "I regret to
disappoint, but our answer remains unchanged. We came
only in search of our sister."

The air tightens. Paris shoves back from the table
and rises sharply.

"We spend our time in vain."

He storms out. His sandals slap against
stone. Then—silence.

"My brother," Hector says with a dry sigh, "ever
the diplomat."

Priam stares after him, eyes flaring. "That boy stirs
a deep fire in me. Pride and selfishness rule him. Troy
teeters by his hand. And he is blind to it."

"When adversity confronts him," Hector adds, "he
tucks his tail and flees with remarkable skill."

Another quiet moment.

Then Priam turns his gaze to Hippolyta.

"If I may… a word of counsel."

Penthesilea watches him now — every muscle still,
senses sharpened like a drawn bow.

"You are queen now," the king says gently. "The

shield and steward of your people. Their safety must weigh above all else. Indulgence is the privilege of poets, not rulers."

He lets the words sink in.

"A lesson Paris has sorely failed to learn."

He leans back again. Penthesilea absorbs the words, her expression unreadable.

Hector speaks again. "Flawed though he may be, he is blood. And he is ours. As we defend Troy, so too shall we defend him."

Hippolyta rises slowly. "The hour grows late. We must prepare for our return."

Penthesilea stands beside her. Hector does the same.

"It is unwise to travel by night," Hector says. "Please... remain until dawn."

"I would welcome a quiet night of rest," Penthesilea admits.

Priam nods, something almost relieved in his features. "Then at sunrise, Hector can show you the true splendor of our city."

Penthesilea glances to Hippolyta. Their eyes meet.

A pause.

A nod.

"Very well," Hippolyta says.

Chapter 21

The valley lies heavy beneath the night sky, quiet and black as oil.

Only scattered campfires mark the Thessalian encampment, their dull orange glow flickering against iron helms and grim faces. Smoke rises lazily into the dark, thick with the scent of charred goat meat and damp leather. The murmurs of tired men ripple through the stillness — low, subdued, more breath than speech.

Hoofbeats echo across the ground like a drumbeat from Hades.

Achilles returns.

He rides at the head of a small band of soldiers, dust clinging to his bronze cuirass, his expression unreadable. At his side, mounted with the grace of a warrior and the defiance of a queen, is Briseis.

The moment they are seen, the hush begins to splinter.

Whistles cut through the quiet. Grunts and jeers follow. Half-drunk soldiers abandon their meals, eyes glinting in the firelight as they catch sight of the woman beside Achilles. The buzz spreads like smoke through dry grass.

She does not flinch.

They arrive before Achilles' tent — a large canvas structure, weathered by war but still regal in its presence.

Achilles dismounts fluidly, tossing the reins over a wooden stake, muscles rippling with precision.

Then, from the gloom, another figure stumbles into view.

King Agamemnon.

The lord of Mycenae emerges from a nearby tent, one hand fumbling with the leather belt around his waist, the other dragging lazily across his chest. His tunic hangs crooked, his cheeks flushed, not from battle but wine. Behind him, a woman — bare-shouldered, breathless — slips into the shadows. Agamemnon doesn't look back.

"What is the meaning of this noise?" he barks, voice thick with drink.

Achilles says nothing. Instead, he turns and lifts Briseis from the saddle with careful strength, setting her on the earth with more grace than any warlord should possess.

Agamemnon takes a step closer.

Then another.

His eyes catch the lines of her face, the torn dress, the dirt smudged across her brow. But it is her bearing — proud, fierce, unyielding — that captures him most.

"And what treasure is this?" he asks, his lips wet and smirking.

"It is of no matter to you," Achilles replies.

The air stills.

Agamemnon reaches out, a slow and presumptuous motion toward Briseis — perhaps to touch her chin, her shoulder, or simply assert ownership.

But before his fingers can reach her, Achilles moves.

Swift.

Final.

He steps between them with the certainty of a man born to defy kings. His shoulders block the firelight. His tone is iron.

"Agamemnon. As I said… no concern of yours."

A long silence.

The two men lock eyes.

Agamemnon, drunk but not unaware, measures the weight behind the words. He sees something in Achilles' gaze — a depth he cannot outdrink, cannot command. A thing far older than rank or title.

Achilles turns his back.

He leads Briseis toward his tent without another word. She follows without hesitation, her chin high, the watching soldiers falling into silence once more as they pass.

Agamemnon lingers in place, one hand still halfway raised, now useless.

He watches them go.

"We shall see," he mutters under his breath, too low for any ears but his own.

But the firelight catches his face — and there is no mistaking the scowl beneath it.

Chapter 22

Morning spills softly into the stone chamber. A golden hue creeps across the floor, catching on polished bronze and the sleek curves of Penthesilea's weaponry, laid out in deliberate order beside her.

She moves through her routine with precision — strapping on leather, inspecting the edge of her sword, tightening the bowstring. Her face is calm, yet there's something practiced in her silence, as if she prepares not just for battle, but to armor her thoughts.

A knock interrupts.

She turns. The door opens.

Hector stands in the threshold, framed by morning light. His smile is gentle, boyish even.

"Are you set?"

Penthesilea shakes her head — not quite no, not quite yes. Just a quiet motion that says: I am not yet sure what I am setting myself for.

The Agora is awake and throbbing with life. Here, noise is a language all its own — the rhythm of hooves, the clash of amphorae, the sing-song cries of merchants who shout their prices with the passion of poets. A dozen languages echo off limestone walls, bargaining, cursing, laughing. Dust lifts in clouds beneath hundreds of feet, mingling with the rich scent of figs and fried honey cakes, fish hauled fresh from the bay, olives crushed into oil.

The square is a churning river of humanity.

Men in embroidered robes haggle with toothless vendors. Young girls weave flower crowns and trail after their mothers, dodging donkeys burdened with jugs. Street musicians pluck lyres, their melodies half-lost beneath the roar. Painted vases glint beneath rows of linen awnings, their glossy surfaces reflecting the sun like flame.

Into this chaos step Penthesilea and Hippolyta, following Hector.

He moves with practiced ease, slipping through the crowd like a blade through cloth. Townspeople part before him, nodding with respect, some placing hands to their hearts. A butcher shouts his name with a grin, offering a fistful of salted lamb. Hector returns each greeting with casual warmth — a wave, a kind word, a smile that seems carved into him.

The Amazons are less at ease.

Hippolyta's gaze darts from stall to stall, the flood of color and sound both dazzling and suspicious. Penthesilea's hand lingers near the hilt of her blade, every instinct trained to read movement, to weigh the intent behind every smile.

"Greetings," Hector offers to a passing artisan, who bows slightly and vanishes into the crowd.

Penthesilea glances at Hippolyta. They share a look — wry, almost disbelieving.

Trojans, it seems, treat their princes like favored

sons of Olympus.

A merchant barrels toward them, bowl cradled in his arms. He bows low, nearly spilling the ripe contents.

"For the lady," he says, beaming at Hippolyta. "Sweet figs. Only the finest."

She eyes the fruit, skeptical. One fig rolls to the edge of the bowl, glistening with nectar. She plucks it delicately, inspects it — then takes a bite.

The change is instant.

Her eyes widen. The tension in her shoulders slips away. "Mmm."

The merchant grins wider. "Come. There is more."

Hippolyta gives her sister a sidelong glance.

"You are in capable hands," she says. "Do not wait on me. I shall come find you."

Before Penthesilea can protest, she's gone — swept into the marketplace's current.

Penthesilea exhales, resigned. Her fingers curl at her side.

Hector chuckles. "As you see… our people are kind and welcoming."

Children rush past, chasing each other with bundles of feathers tied to sticks. One nearly clips Hector's leg; he sidesteps without breaking stride.

"Certainly not deserving of harm," he adds quietly. His tone is casual, but Penthesilea hears the deeper note beneath it — the diplomatic plea, wrapped in charm. They walk on.

Beyond the Agora, the city stills. The shouts grow distant, swallowed by stone alleys and the hush of shaded arcades. Here, the housing district lives in simplicity. Homes of whitewashed stone sit nestled together, humble but clean. Vines twist up their walls, and drying herbs hang from every balcony. The fragrance of thyme and rosemary lingers in the warm air.

Penthesilea and Hector walk in measured silence.

"I have learned much of your city," she says, "but —"

"May I speak plainly?" he interrupts.

She nods. "Always."

"For one so fair…" He chooses his words carefully. "You wield a blade as though blessed by Ares himself."

Penthesilea lifts an eyebrow, unimpressed.

"For one so fair? That is the measure of my worth?"

He raises his hands, surrendering with a grin.

"Forgive me. You have misunderstood."

A pause.

"I watched you spar with Theseus yesterday. I was well impressed."

He reaches out, fingers brushing her forearm — light, deliberate.

"Achilles would underestimate you. That would grant you an edge."

She draws back — not sharply, but decisively.

"As much as I would relish the slaying of Greeks, Hippolyta has made our path clear. We shall not join your war."

She glances toward the city, its rooftops red with sun.

"Even the beauty of your city will not sway her. Yet I have never seen her stir as she did before the offerings of that merchant."

A rare smile breaks her stillness. Hector returns it.

They pause beneath the woven canopy of a quiet garden, where a fountain murmurs behind stone walls. Bees move lazily from flower to flower, unbothered by the world's impending violence.

"Very well," Hector says.

"May I ask you something?" Penthesilea asks.

"Of course."

"Have you ever stood at a crossroads… between what your heart desires and what your duty demands… though it meant breaking a promise you once made?"

The words carry weight — not just curiosity, but confession.

Hector's expression stills.

"I have."

His voice lowers.

"Such choices cut deeper than any spear."

He continues.

"Perhaps the truer question is… if your soul finds no peace, how can it rise to become all you are meant to be?"

His words hang in the air like incense — soft but penetrating.

Penthesilea says nothing.

But her gaze lingers on him.

And for once, her silence does not seem like armor.

The afternoon sun burns low in the sky, casting a golden hue across the gates of Troy. Dust stirs beneath the hooves of the horses, the scent of sweat and leather hanging in the heat. The walls of the city rise behind them — proud, ancient, bearing the scars of siege and time alike.

Hippolyta sits tall astride her steed, a portrait of command and grace. Her dark braid coils over one shoulder, the points of her bronze armor glinting like flame. Eyes narrowed, she watches the horizon, ever alert.

Nearby, Hector — prince of Troy, warrior of unmatched discipline — steps forward to offer a steadying hand as Penthesilea mounts her horse. There is no need for it, and she makes that known.

"Your aid was not required."

"Courtesy. Nothing more," he replies, voice calm as still water, but edged with quiet pride.

From the side, Hippolyta scoffs, a breath of amusement barely hidden beneath her poise. A knowing smile teases the corner of her mouth.

"Of course it is," she mutters under her breath, just loud enough for herself.

Hector, undisturbed, hands each Amazon a small satchel — leather, laced with simple embroidery. The weight of practical generosity.

"A few provisions for your journey home."

Hippolyta opens hers with a glance — dried fruits,

cured meats, bandages, a small flask. Sustenance and forethought.

"That is generous of you," Penthesilea says, her tone even, unreadable.

"Yes. Thank you," Hippolyta adds, a rare softness in her voice.

A silence follows, but it is not empty. It hums with something unspoken.

Penthesilea meets Hector's gaze. For a breath, they do not move — two warriors bound by shared respect, something deeper pulsing beneath their iron skins. The breeze stirs Penthesilea's dark hair across her cheek. Neither breaks the gaze.

Until Hippolyta clears her throat — the moment shatters like a dropped blade.

"We should be on our way."

She spurs her horse gently, the beast lurching into motion toward the city gates. Penthesilea follows, though her head turns — one final glance cast over her shoulder.

Hector raises a hand in farewell, a faint smile lingering on his lips. He does not speak of what passes between them. He lets it settle into memory.

"It was a pleasure," he calls, his voice almost swallowed by the wind.

And then — distant horns.

Low and mournful, they echo across the plains beyond Troy's walls.

Something is coming.

CHAPTER 23

Dust and tension swirl in equal measure across the Thessalian plain. Beneath the blistering midday sun, the Greek encampment stirs like a beehive rattled. Bronze glints in rhythmic flashes as Myrmidons, Spartans, and Mycenaeans hone their blades and beat the dents from their battered shields. The scent of sweat, leather, and anticipation is thick in the air — the kind of oppressive stillness that descends before blood spills.

Menelaus of Sparta walks through the war-bent chaos, his jaw set, lips a tight line. He is still young, not yet thirty, but already wearied by too many battles, too much pride. Beside him, Odysseus of Ithaca moves like a shadow — older, sharper, always thinking three steps ahead. Neither man speaks. Their silence carries weight, their expressions grim as they pass through the army of restless warriors preparing for war.

Inside Agamemnon's tent, the air is hot, close, and perfumed faintly with wine and something fouler — the stink of power misused.

Agamemnon, High King of the Greeks, lounges over Briseis as if she were a feast spread for his pleasure. One arm slung possessively around her, the other cradling a half-full cup, he presses close. Briseis, priestess and prize, recoils beneath his hand, disgust and defiance mingling in her eyes.

"Let go of me, you boar."

Her voice is sharp, but Agamemnon only smirks, amused by her resistance, as if her protest is just another part of the game.

A voice slices through the tent's heavy silence.

"Brother?"

Agamemnon straightens, his amusement vanishing. Menelaus enters, Odysseus close behind. They do not wait for permission.

Briseis slips free of Agamemnon's grasp, melting into the tent's shadows like a wraith. Her presence lingers, palpable and watchful. The air tightens with something volatile.

Agamemnon exhales, composing himself.

"As you can see, Menelaus, I am occupied. What is it you want?"

Menelaus' eyes flick toward the figure now half-veiled in shadow.

"Is that not the girl Achilles took from Lyrnessus?"

He gestures. Agamemnon nods with pride. Odysseus, behind him, shakes his head slowly, weary of the path unfolding.

"I see you were swift to act."

Agamemnon steps forward, shoulders squared.

"What do you imply?"

The air carries the heavy musk of wine. Menelaus wrinkles his nose and eyes the mug in his brother's hand.

"Odysseus… tell him what you have just told me."

Odysseus speaks plainly.

"Achilles declared he will not fight with us. He offered no reason, but his intent was clear."

"She is why," Menelaus says, motioning toward Briseis, her eyes watching from the shadows.

A pause.

"Odysseus asked him to stand with us. And this... is your gratitude?"

Agamemnon's jaw tightens. His grip on the mug shifts.

"You could not hold your hand until Troy lay in ruin?"

"You know I am not a man who waits easily,"Agamemnon says with a slight growl.

He turns toward Briseis again, his gaze smoldering with unearned entitlement.

"Even I am not free of desire."

Briseis recoils from the attention. Her face reveals nothing but the depths of her contempt.

Odysseus speaks, more command than plea.

"Return her at once and Achilles will overlook your offense."

"You must return her," Menelaus echoes, his voice firm.

Agamemnon's voice snaps like a drawn bowstring.

"Mind your tongue. She will remain here."

Menelaus is unmoved.

"He is unmatched in battle. Without him, how do you intend we defeat the Trojans?"

"Our victory does not rest upon him."

"If you believe that, then you are more of a fool than when I entered."

Agamemnon's cup flies through the air, crashing against a marble pillar, shattering. Wine stains the stone like blood.

"Listen, little brother. Achilles is but a man... like you and I."

Menelaus' voice turns low, almost venomous.

"Lest you forget, he is born of a goddess. He is only half mortal... more than I can say of you, on your best day."

His eyes drift to Briseis once more. She stares back, a statue of silent defiance.

"Careful. Brother."

"We need him."

Agamemnon's response drips with sarcasm.

"If you believe that, then I must concede you are the greater fool."

Menelaus glares. With a sweep of his cloak, he turns and storms out. Odysseus follows, silent and watchful.

Within another tent, quieter but no less charged, Achilles lies entangled with Patroclus. They rest in the warmth of shared stillness, the intimacy between them not spoken, only lived. Sheets are half-kicked aside. A low light filters in from the tent's flap, casting soft shadows across sun-burnished skin.

Patroclus speaks, voice low with restrained worry.

"Are you certain you do not wish to join the war? I

know how greatly battle calls you."

Achilles exhales slowly, eyes to the ceiling.

"What would you have me do? Agamemnon took what was mine."

"It has not yet been a full day. Does she truly matter so much?"

His voice cracks, more emotion than question. Achilles doesn't look at him.

"You know it is not the girl. It is the insult."

Patroclus sits up, the words weighing heavy between them.

Then — intrusion.

The tent flap bursts open. Menelaus and Odysseus stand in the opening, caught abruptly in the intimacy they've shattered.

A long, stunned silence.

"Achilles," Odysseus says with brisk formality. "I shall wait outside."

He withdraws quickly. Menelaus remains, shifting his stance.

"Forgive the intrusion. I hope I did not—"

"You did."

Achilles cuts him off, eyes sharp. Patroclus rises, wrapping a linen sheet around his waist. Menelaus averts his eyes quickly, awkward in his discomfort.

Achilles stands slowly, pulling a cloak over himself, the movement deliberate.

"What is it you want, Menelaus?"

"I have been told—"

"You can turn around."

Menelaus obeys, stiff and quiet.

"I understand you no longer intend to fight with us. Having just left Agamemnon, I know your reason. Is there aught I may do to sway you?"

Achilles steps forward until their faces are a breath apart. Patroclus, from across the tent, watches like a coiled spring.

"Have your brother return Briseis to me."

"I tried."

"And failed. Clearly."

"I was not made to kneel."

"Nor was I."

Menelaus' voice dips, less prideful now. "It is not wise to press this war forward without you."

A faint, wry smile flickers across Achilles' face. He turns his back.

"I am here as a courtesy to Odysseus. I owe this war nothing. Your brother even less."

A pause, then steel in his voice.

"Until she is returned, neither I nor the Myrmidons shall lift a sword."

He turns again, gaze hard.

"And he must offer an apology for the insult he dealt... before the men. Before the gods."

Menelaus exhales, beaten down by pride and logic alike. The silence wraps around them like fog.

Patroclus speaks, breaking through it.

"Then I shall go. I will take up arms and lead our

men."

The words explode in the tent like thrown spearpoints. Achilles turns sharply. Menelaus does too.

"You shall not," Achilles growls.

"I shall. You cannot stop me."

Menelaus, uncertain, interjects with quiet urgency.

"We depart tonight... When the moon sits highest in the sky."

Achilles crosses the space between them in a single step, nose to nose with Patroclus. The tension is fire— sparking, flaring, dangerous.

"You cannot shield me from fate forever," Patroclus says. "I shall do this... with or without your blessing."

"This is about that girl, is it not?"

"I am amused by how small you think of me."

Achilles studies him, eyes hard, heart pulled in two directions.

"No. I forbid it."

Patroclus turns on his heel, vanishing into the night like a storm unchained. Menelaus hesitates — then, with a slight nod, follows.

Inside the tent, Achilles stands alone. Still. Burning.

Chapter 24

The night stretches across the Thessalian valley like a veil of polished obsidian. Above, the moon hovers near full — a luminous disc bathing the black waters of the Aegean in ghostly silver. Its reflection flickers across the waves like scattered coins, and the endless line of Greek ships lies beached along the shore like slumbering beasts, their masts rising like spears against the night sky.

On the sand, warriors from Sparta, Mycenae, and Ithaca move with hushed precision. Cloaks drawn tight against the salt wind, they tighten sails, check blades, secure bundles of dried meat and water skins. Their hands work without hesitation — men seasoned by campaign, accustomed to the rituals of war. The sea whispers to them like a god of fate, always watching, always pulling forward.

But in the shadowy heart of the camp, the Myrmidons remain still.

Dark as obsidian and silent as tombs, they sleep beneath their worn leathers and bronze helms, loyal to one man and one cause. Their weapons lie untouched. Their ships wait, sails slack, oars lashed. For without Achilles, they do not stir.

Inside the flickering half-light of his tent, Achilles watches.

He stands near the flap, the soft leather brushing

against his arm, gazing out at the preparations with unreadable eyes. His silhouette is carved by the firelight, broad-shouldered, still. The camp beyond lives and breathes, but he remains apart — a storm withheld.

From across the space, a voice.

"I still wish to sail with the Greeks."

Patroclus. His voice does not tremble, though the air between them is strained, stretched taut by something neither of them says aloud.

Achilles turns, slowly.

Patroclus stands with arms at his sides, expression resolute — no longer the quiet companion or shadow, but a man with his own will forged in fire. His tunic clings to him from the heat of the tent; his hair damp with sweat, but his eyes are clear, unblinking.

"Why such haste to leave?" Achilles asks, his voice low.

"I seek to understand the honor you strive for."

Achilles steps forward. Firelight dances across his bare chest, muscles tense beneath skin bronzed from battle and sun. There's conflict in his eyes, flickering like flame — not anger, not yet. Worry, perhaps. Fear cloaked in pride.

"If I may speak plainly..." he begins, then pauses.

"You are not prepared."

Stillness. Silence. Outside, a gull cries in the dark.

Patroclus does not flinch.

"Is that truly what you believe?" he says. "Or is it you who is not prepared?"

The words hang heavy in the air, weighted like

iron.

Achilles' jaw hardens. A muscle twitches along his cheek. He does not reply.

"Excuse me," he says at last.

Without another word, he brushes past Patroclus, his shoulder catching lightly against the other man's as he exits the tent. His presence lingers behind like a wave receding — tension and warmth and something breaking beneath the surface.

Inside, the fire crackles.

Its orange glow flickers across the objects left behind — the rough-hewn furniture, the shield propped against the wall, and the armor.

Achilles' armor.

It sits in a carved wooden chair like a relic, burnished bronze gleaming in the light. The breastplate is star-speckled, chased with constellations inlaid by a master's hand. It is beautiful and terrible — the garb of a demigod, worn by a man who has never been just a man.

Patroclus stares at it, breath catching. His gaze is drawn to it like the tide to the moon.

He crosses the space. Slowly at first, then with purpose. His hand trembles, only once.

He seizes the armor.

The Aegean stretches out beneath a sky of hammered silver.

A thousand ships slice through the dark waters, their hulls cutting clean lines into the tide. Rowers move in harmony, oars rising and falling in rhythm — a thousand arms pulling toward fate.

At the bow of one sleek trireme, figures stand as shadows against the starlight.

Menelaus, stern and brooding. Agamemnon, proud as ever, cloaked in arrogance and victory not yet won. Odysseus, quiet, his sharp eyes reading more than he says. And with them — gleaming under the pale moonlight — stands Patroclus.

The armor of Achilles fits him like a second skin. Bright bronze, star-forged, unmistakable. He does not speak, but the illusion speaks for him. The men around him believe.

Menelaus turns to him, voice carried low beneath the wind.

"I am grateful you persuaded him to reconsider."

"He only required rest," Patroclus replies, his voice controlled. "He woke in better spirits."

"His armor suits you."

Patroclus offers a tight smile, eyes forward, locked on the horizon.

Behind them, the oars churn. Sea spray glistens in the moonlight like shattered glass.

Agamemnon smirks, careless.

"You see? All that concern... for nothing."

Menelaus casts him a cold glance — sharp, unforgiving.

"We are stronger with Achilles. When we return, you will make amends."

Odysseus raises an eyebrow, half-amused.

"I admire your confidence, Menelaus. Though I would wager better on our return if the true son of Thetis sailed beside us."

"We shall fare well," Agamemnon insists. "And when victory is ours, so too shall be Troy."

Menelaus' reply comes without hesitation, his voice flint.

"Troy means nothing to me. It is Helen I seek."

Agamemnon's hand claps onto his brother's shoulder, heavy with mock affection.

"My brother... driven by one desire and blind to all else."

"She is all that matters."

"Be that as it may," Agamemnon says, smirking, "the end remains the same. And I await with great eagerness."

The wind picks up, carrying the ships forward — toward blood, toward legacy, toward the fate none of them can yet name.

Chapter 25

The forest glows with the soft gold of dawn. Sunlight spills through ancient trees in cascading beams, and birdsong fills the canopy in delicate harmony. The earth is damp with morning dew. Leaves rustle softly beneath hooves as Penthesilea and Hippolyta ride beneath the vaulting green, sisters once more — united by blood, bound now by choice.

Their mounts move in rhythm, a graceful procession beneath the cathedral of nature.

"That Prince Hector appeared quite taken with you," Hippolyta says, a faint tease threading her tone.

Penthesilea's jaw tenses.

"He sees only my beauty. Nothing more."

"Is that so terrible?"

Penthesilea pulls her reins, her mare halting among the shafts of light. Hippolyta does the same, watching her sister with quiet patience.

"You know that is not the sort of admiration I seek."

"Must it weigh so heavily?"

The breeze hushes. The forest stills. Even the birds seem to listen.

"Why are we speaking of this?" Penthesilea murmurs.

A hush falls. The green world around them waits.

"Beauty is a strength," Hippolyta says. "Yet you wear it like a burden."

Penthesilea considers this in silence.

"If I may speak freely," Hippolyta continues, "I have long envied your beauty."

"You need not flatter me."

"It is true. That... and the bond you shared with Mother. She favored you."

Penthesilea's voice softens, threading truth through vulnerability.

"Curious. I envied you."

A pause.

"Firstborn. First to wield a sword. First to wear the crown."

A shared laugh breaks the tension like a branch snapping underfoot — gentle, unexpected, familiar.

"Strange, is it not?" Hippolyta says. "The heart longs most for what it has never held."

Her voice dips.

"And yet, it was the sister between us who drew us close."

"Then let me speak plainly..." Penthesilea says, a fierce light in her eyes. "As a daughter of Otrera, I shall do my part. I will stand beside you. What our mother built — I will uphold."

"It is what she would have wished."

"I am glad to hear it," Hippolyta replies. "I did not expect we would come to such an accord."

"Nor did I," Penthesilea admits. "Perhaps the

king's counsel swayed me. Or perhaps it was this journey. Antiope. You. Regardless, I see now... My place is with you. With Themyscira."

"You speak with clarity. I welcome it."

She reaches for her sister's hand — warrior's grasp to warrior's grasp.

"You shall take Antiope's place and command our army. I have always known you to be the strongest among us."

A crooked smile rises.

"If only there were a way to temper your stubbornness."

Penthesilea smirks as Hippolyta opens Hector's satchel and peers inside.

"The bag is empty," Hippolyta grumbles. "And I am famished."

"As am I. A hunt, then?"

"Let us compete, as we once did."

"Have your wounds healed fully?"

"The gift of divine blood," Hippolyta replies with a shrug, flexing easily atop her horse.

"Good. I prefer no excuses when I best you."

They dismount in tandem, movements fluid and well-practiced. Penthesilea reaches for her bow, but Hippolyta stops her.

"Spears only."

Intrigued, Penthesilea arches a brow.

"What do you have in mind?"

In the hush beneath the canopy, the forest shifts. A twig snaps. Both sisters freeze.

A doe steps into the clearing, its coat a burnished gold in the morning light. It lifts its head, nostrils flaring, eyes wide.

Penthesilea and Hippolyta trade glances. Mischief dances silently between them.

"Loser cleans the kill," Penthesilea whispers.

"And what task falls to me?" Hippolyta murmurs back.

Penthesilea scoffs.

Far across the land, Troy's beaches roar with war.

A thousand ships line the shore, dark and unrelenting. Greek soldiers pour onto the sand in wave after wave, shields lifted, spears gleaming beneath the rising sun. The sea churns behind them, and fate stands ahead.

At the front, Menelaus, Odysseus, and Agamemnon gaze toward the gates.

And beside them — radiant in bronze, helm tucked under one arm — stands Patroclus, hidden behind the armor of Achilles.

His eyes are focused, his breath calm, but every step is borrowed valor.

"At last," Agamemnon breathes.

The doe crashes through the brush, lithe and luminous, a streak of motion and fear. Dew flies from her hooves. Her ribs heave. She zigzags through twisted roots and shafts of golden light.

Penthesilea veers left, vaulting over a moss-covered log with predator grace. Her eyes are narrowed, her lips parted just slightly to drink the wind. Branches tear at her arms, vines coil and snap, but she doesn't slow.

To the right, Hippolyta moves through the woods like a striking hawk. Her legs pump hard, breath coming sharp. Each step is memory: the races as children, the duels in training, the weight of their mother's gaze. The thrill of pursuit floods her blood. Her spear is poised in her grip, balanced perfectly for the throw.

They flank the creature like stormfronts.

Far away, beyond forest and sea, Troy roars awake to the sound of steel and fury.

At the gates, the clash begins.

Spears shatter. Bronze slams against wood. The ground shudders beneath the weight of thousands. The Greeks pour forward, formation breaking into blood-frothed chaos. Screams rise — first from the dying, then from those who live long enough to witness.

Hector rides through it all like a god on foot, dismounting with fluid finality. His boots crush blood-soaked sand as he carves through two Greeks without hesitation. His blade glides cleanly, practiced. Unforgiving. He moves toward the heart of it — toward the weight in his gut that pulls him forward.

In the forest, the doe stumbles once.

A stone turns beneath her hoof. She falters, recovers, sprints on — but not fast enough.

Her breath comes in short, shallow bursts. Her muscles quiver. Her ears flick. She is close to breaking.

Penthesilea sees her opening. She drops into a crouch behind a sloping rock, her body stilling like a drawn bow. Her spear slides into her palm, smooth and certain. Her heartbeat slows. All the noise — birdsong, wind, memory — fades.

"Easy," she whispers.

To her left, Hippolyta slows as well, watching from behind a cedar. Her brow furrows in concentration. Her own breath catches, and a strange unease tugs at her ribs. She adjusts her grip without thinking.

Across the plain, Hector sees him.

That gleam of bronze. That silhouette —
undeniable.
Achilles.

He stands over a fallen Trojan, bathed in morning light and shadow. But there's something wrong. The stance. The movement.

The doubt is fleeting, but it burns.

"Achilles..." Hector murmurs, almost to himself.

He sees a spear on the ground. Wood, raw and worn from use. He bends. Picks it up. Feels its weight. Cold and familiar.

Penthesilea's arm rises.

The wind shifts, silent.

Hector's arm rises.

No sound, no thought.

Two warriors. Two fates.

They throw.

The spears cut the air like judgment.

On the battlefield, Patroclus sees nothing until the impact hits him like the sky falling.

The spear tears through armor, through flesh, through breath.

He buckles, stunned, and the ground rushes toward him. The helmet slips from his head as he crumples. Bronze rolls to the sand. His eyes are wide — not with pain, but surprise.

Menelaus is already there, sprinting across the carnage. He falls to his knees, hands trembling as he lifts the helmet away.

It is not Achilles.

It is the boy.

The boy who rode beside the hero. Who shared his tent. His bed. His life.

"Patroclus," he breathes.

The wind howls.

In the forest, the doe jerks once, then falls.

Penthesilea's spear pierces it clean through, buried to the haft. The animal slumps silently, the forest hushed in reverence.

She rises, triumphant. Her chest lifts with pride, but her hands shake ever so slightly. Not with effort — with awe. The kill was perfect.

She turns to call out—

"Hippolyta!"

Penthesilea cups her hands around her mouth, voice bounding between trees. She sprints toward the fallen doe, heart still pounding from the thrill of the chase.

"Sister!"

She kneels beside the animal, fingers tracing the clean wound.

"It is done. At last, I have bested you."

She laughs, bright and unguarded.

"Do you hear me, Hippolyta?"

Silence answers.

She straightens slowly. The trees seem too still. The light has grown colder.

"Hippolyta? You can come out now. The challenge is over. I won."

Nothing.

Her breath quickens. She turns in a slow circle, eyes scanning.

"Hippolyta?"

She begins to walk, following the imagined path of the spear. Her feet crunch leaves that now sound too loud in the silence.

Then she sees it.

And stops.

The world tilts.

Her spear is buried in Hippolyta's chest.

"No."

She crashes to her knees beside her sister, blood soaking the forest floor, soaking her hands.

"Hippolyta," she chokes. "No, no, no—"

Hippolyta's eyes flutter open.

"Penthe—"

"Shhh. Save your strength."

She cradles her gently, trying to stop the bleeding, trying to unmake what has happened. The spear's wound is deep, too deep. Blood seeps between her fingers, hot and fast.

"I love you," Penthesilea whispers. "I am so sorry. I did not mean—"

"I forgive you."

Hippolyta smiles. It's soft. Tired. Real.

Then she exhales — and does not breathe again.

Her hand slips from her sister's cheek, falling to the earth beside a single red anemone.

Penthesilea clutches her sister's body, rocking, the sound that escapes her throat not quite human.

"Hippolyta..."

There is no reply. Only the hush of trees.

"Why?" she whispers. "How much more must be taken?"

Her cry splits the stillness, shattering dawn.

Chapter 26

The air inside Achilles' tent is thick — not with heat or incense, but with grief, sharp and unbearable. Shadows gather in corners where the fire dares not flicker. The canvas walls close in like tombstones.

Achilles screams.

It is not the cry of a warrior, but something far more ancient — the sound of love torn from the world. He clutches Patroclus' body as if he can will it back to breath, to warmth. His fingers are blood-streaked, trembling, pressed to skin already beginning to cool.

His mouth opens again, but the scream has hollowed him. All that comes is breath.

Menelaus stands nearby, silent. Odysseus is beside him, jaw locked, his eyes flicking between the ground and the dead boy. They do not know where to look — there is no right place. The tent itself seems to shudder under the weight of what it holds.

"Achilles, I—" Menelaus begins, his voice ragged.

Achilles lifts a hand. A single gesture.

He doesn't look up, doesn't speak. Just a shake of the head.

That's enough.

Menelaus glances at Odysseus. They exchange a look. Neither needs words. Quietly, they step out into the night.

Outside, the camp is quieter than it should be.

The injured shuffle between tents with the help of others. Bronze armor clinks faintly, water is ladled from bowls. The usual murmur of soldier's talk is dimmed — as if the wind itself dares not carry laughter tonight.

A handful of men stand outside the tent, waiting. They do not speak.

Achilles emerges.

His face is pale, expressionless. His eyes, once fire, are now empty stone.

In his arms, he carries Patroclus.

No one stops him. No one dares.

He walks past them, step by step, into the falling light.

Far beyond the Greek camp, in the flickering warmth of dusk, Hector sits among his officers. A dozen men gathered around a low fire, a fresh-killed boar roasting above the flame. Their faces are tired, leather-skinned and war-hardened, but tonight there is levity.

"To you, Prince Hector," one of them says, raising a cup. "You have greatly weakened the Greeks."

Hector leans back slightly, eyes reflecting the firelight. A curl of smoke drifts from the meat, rising into the darkening sky.

"I expected more from Achilles," he says with a scoff. "Given his legend."

"In the end, he was but a man," another officer

mutters, and laughter follows.

But Hector doesn't join in.

"Perhaps," he replies, standing with an apple in his hand. "Still, much work remains."

He bites into the fruit — crisp, loud in the quiet moment. Juice runs down his wrist as he turns from the fire.

"Tell the men to rest well," he says. "This war is far from over."

"With you leading, the end draws near," someone calls after him. "Victory is within reach."

He doesn't reply, but a smirk touches his lips as he walks into the growing dark.

Along the cliffs above the Thessalian Valley, where sea meets sky in a blur of dusk, Achilles kneels.

His knees press into the coarse brush. His armor lies behind him, discarded. The wind claws at his hair and cloak, but he doesn't feel it.

Before him lies Patroclus — his limbs straightened, eyes gently closed, hair pushed from his brow with trembling reverence.

Achilles looks up. The sky offers no answer.

His head falls back and he releases a scream — raw, guttural, wordless. It rips from his throat like the tearing of flesh, echoing off stone and sea, swallowed by the endless horizon.

No warrior's cry. No prayer to the gods.

Just grief.

CHAPTER 27

The flames rise high into the Themysciran sky, painting the night in hues of gold and blood.

Hippolyta lies atop the pyre, her face serene in death. Her armor gleams softly beneath the firelight, still regal, still commanding — a queen to the very end. The wood beneath her cracks and groans as it burns, the smoke winding skyward like a prayer none dare speak aloud.

Around her, the Amazons form a solemn circle. No voice breaks the silence. Their stillness is not restraint — it is reverence.

At the front of the gathering, Penthesilea stands with Melanippe. Their hands clutch each other's as the fire climbs.

The heat touches their skin, but neither moves. The flames reflect in Penthesilea's eyes — two endless infernos mirrored in her own.

She does not blink.

She does not breathe.

Something inside her begins to unravel.

Time blurs. Grief reigns.

Penthesilea is crowned queen.

She kneels before the altar of Otrera and Hippolyta, hands shaking, eyes downcast. The ceremonial circlet is laid upon her brow — a circlet that once crowned the proudest of queens, now resting on the head of a woman shattered from within.

The Amazons cheer, but their voices are distant, echoes wrapped in fog. She hears nothing. Feels nothing.

Only the absence.

Only the hollow where Hippolyta once stood.

Days pass.

Nights blend.

She does not rise.

Melanippe sits beside her, arms around her shoulders. Thyra kneels at her feet. They speak softly, but Penthesilea stares ahead, unblinking.

Her eyes no longer move. They remain fixed on some point far beyond the walls, beyond the island, beyond the world.

Thyra tries to feed her.

She presses bread into Penthesilea's hands, lifts a cup to her lips, but the queen's mouth remains closed. Her fingers do not curl. Her throat does not swallow.

Only silence.

Thyra sings to her at dusk — a low, mournful hymn passed down by the river-keepers. It is not the lullaby of old, but something older still, rooted in grief and ash. The melody winds through the stone chambers, curling around torches and shadows.

Penthesilea does not react. She sits like marble, her posture regal, her soul absent.

The song ends.

The silence deepens.

Melanippe bathes her.

Warm water steams around them as she runs a cloth down her sister's back, whispering small comforts. She speaks of Themyscira, of duties left undone, of memories half-remembered. But Penthesilea's face does not move. Her skin shivers from cold that isn't in the room.

Her body is present.

Her spirit has gone to where her sister walks — somewhere unreachable.

In her sleeping quarters, Penthesilea lies still.

Sweat clings to her skin. Her hair is damp, fanned out across her pillow like tangled night.

Beside her, Thyra watches in silence. She dips a cloth in a bowl of water, wrings it out, and presses it gently to Penthesilea's brow. The gesture is patient. Loving. Desperate.

The fire in the brazier flickers low. Shadows dance on stone.

Melanippe enters, carrying a tray — simple bread and broth. Her face is lined with worry. She sets the tray down quietly.

"Has she not yet awakened?"

Thyra shakes her head.

Melanippe crosses to the bed, hovering. Her voice is a hush.

"Two moons, and not a flutter. Worry begins to take hold."

Thyra drops the cloth into the basin. The splash is loud in the quiet room.

"Perhaps she has fallen ill," Melanippe says.

Then — movement.

Penthesilea stirs.

Both women freeze.

Her breath hitches. Her back arches. Her hands jerk as if drowning in sleep.

Then — her body convulses, and she sits bolt upright, drenched in sweat.

A scream bursts from her lips — jagged, primal, sharp as a drawn blade. Her eyes are wide, unfocused, darting across the room as though she does not recognize it.

Thyra lunges forward, grabbing her gently by the arms.

"Shhh... Shhh... You are safe."

Penthesilea gasps, her breath ragged and desperate, as if the air has turned to flame.

Melanippe approaches, cautious, hands raised in calm.

"Penthesilea... what is it you seek?"

The queen's eyes flick to her.

One word escapes.

"Hippolyta."

Melanippe closes her eyes - the moment weighing on her. When they open again, they're full of sorrow.

"Do you not remember?"

Silence.

Penthesilea's gaze drifts. A long pause. Her breath slows.

Then —

Clarity strikes like a blade.

Her shoulders crumple. Her frame collapses forward into Thyra's arms. The sob breaks out of her suddenly — small, raw, unformed. It is not a queen's grief, but a child's. It lasts only a moment.

Then it is gone.

She pulls away, jaw set.

Without another word, she storms from the chamber.

Melanippe rushes to follow. She pauses in the doorway, the firelight catching the sheen of unshed tears.

"Penthesilea."

But the queen is already gone — swallowed by shadow, moving toward something only she understands.

Chapter 28

Dawn breaks cold over the Thessalian Valley.

The once-lush expanse now lies brittle and colorless, a bone-dry stretch of earth scoured by wind and war. Shrubs that once blossomed beneath the spring sun have faded to ash-gray skeletons, and the morning breeze carries with it not the scent of salt or life, but dust — and omen. The land reflects its warriors: stripped, raw, waiting for the final blow.

Inside his tent, Achilles prepares.

There is no fire burning, no warmth to speak of — only silence, vast and heavy.

Achilles sits before his armor, the bronze breastplate gleaming dully in the muted light.

He tightens each strap with mechanical precision. The greaves. The bracers. The sword belt. One after the other. His face remains blank, but the tension is there — buried in the muscles of his jaw, in the way he binds each piece as if tying shut an old wound that won't stop bleeding.

There is no hesitation.

Only purpose.

Outside, the wind howls low across the valley like the voice of some forgotten god.

Menelaus waits, his shoulders squared, cloak pressed tight against his armor. Around him, the camp stirs slowly — murmurs in the wind, banners fluttering, soldiers rising like ghosts from their tents. The morning feels unnatural. Hollow.

Achilles steps into the light.

He does not look at Menelaus. He does not slow.

Menelaus falls into step beside him.

"Are the ships ready?" Achilles asks, his voice low but sharp. Like drawn steel.

"They are," Menelaus replies.

They walk, the gravel crunching beneath their feet. Behind them, the silence of the camp thickens.

Achilles' gaze remains forward, locked on something beyond the horizon — something only he sees.

"Hector is mine alone," he says. "Let every man know it."

Menelaus halts, startled by the weight of the words. Achilles does not.

He keeps walking, cloak sweeping behind him like a shadow loosed.

The sky hangs still above them, pale and waiting.

CHAPTER 29

Dusk casts its shadow over Themyscira, and the once-vibrant forest is now a cold cathedral of silence. The canopy overhead dims to a bruised violet, filtering the last light of day into ashen hues. Trees stand like sentinels, motionless. Not a bird sings. Not a creature stirs. Even the wind seems to hold its breath.

Penthesilea wanders alone through the undergrowth.

She is gaunt, pale as parchment, her once-golden skin now sallow and lifeless. Her gait is broken, uneven, as though her bones have forgotten how to carry her. The hem of her chiton is torn and muddy. Her hair, unbraided and wild, hangs in a matted curtain across her face. The forest seems to recoil with each faltering step she takes, as if nature itself mourns with her.

She trips. Falls.

A grunt escapes her lips as her knees hit the earth. She lies there for a breath, unmoving. Then, a glimmer — something pale catches her eye at the base of a tree. Hemlock.

A flicker stirs in her eyes. Not hope. Not fear. Recognition.

Crawling forward on trembling hands and knees, she reaches the small plant, its white buds delicate against the decaying leaves. Her fingers close around it. She plucks one bloom and eats it without hesitation.

The bitterness floods her mouth. The forest twists.

Colors bleed. The bark on the trees undulates, the leaves curl in unnatural rhythm. Wind tears through the branches with a sharpness like blades. Her breath hitches. A speck of light dances past the corner of her eye.

"Who is there?" she whispers, voice hoarse and cracking.

She spins, unsteady. Nothing.

Another bloom. She tears it from the stalk and swallows.

The light returns — quicker now, a pale blur that circles her like a predator.

"You could devour every root in this forest," comes a voice, smooth and low, feminine and merciless, "and still death would not come."

Penthesilea lurches upright, heart hammering. Her sword slides free of its sheath, though her hands tremble.

"Show yourself."

Another voice — colder, flatter: "She does not yet see."

"Leave me be," Penthesilea says, lowering the sword. Her hand flies to her belt. She yanks the knife free and lifts it to her throat.

"Let me perish in peace."

"All your life," the first voice replies, circling, "you have chased the honor of the sword. Why choose silence now?"

Penthesilea closes her eyes. "There is nothing left of

the life I knew. I have lost more than I can carry."

A sudden pulse of shadow rolls across the forest floor.

The Erinyes appear.

Three figures emerge from darkness — not women, not beasts, but something in between. Their hair writhes with serpents. Their eyes burn crimson and unblinking. Wings, ragged and black, stretch behind them like thunderclouds. In their hands: scourges.

"You bring shame to the name you carry," says Megaera.

"Otrera would weep at the sight of you," Tisiphone hisses. "Hippolyta would turn away."

"She is weak," Alecto spits. "She will not do it."

"I will," Penthesilea replies.

She draws a long breath and presses the blade to her throat.

A slice.

A sharp bead of blood wells, slides downward.

She drops the knife. Waits.

Still breathing.

A low chuckle drifts through the trees — not from the Erinyes. A man's laugh, dark and knowing.

Panic flashes in her eyes.

She grabs the blade again and plunges it into her abdomen.

Her chiton darkens with red. She gasps, staggering.

Still breathing.

The forest howls. Wind rises like a scream. Leaves

twist into a cyclone around her. Dirt lashes her skin. She drops to her knees, hands over her ears.

"Make it stop!" she cries.

Lightning rips the sky. Thunder bellows.

Above her, the Dog Star pulses, swells—too bright, too close. A blinding white light erupts, and from within it

—

"Hermes," comes a voice like an avalanche. "Enough."

Stillness falls.

The Erinyes dissolve. Their forms scatter into ash.

In their place, a figure steps from the trees. Slender. Regal. Winged sandals, golden diadem, and staff in hand. Hermes. He says nothing. Only watches.

Then the Dog Star shatters.

From its explosion of light emerges Ares.

Tall. Bare-chested. A red cloak, ember-edged, trails behind him like war itself. His spear crackles with lightning. His shield glows with the heat of a forge. His eyes are flame.

And then—darkness.

The forest dims again, as if nothing had changed.

"Leave her," Ares commands, voice thunderous. "Find someone else to torment."

Hermes blurs, golden and gone.

Ares lands. The ground splits beneath his feet.

Penthesilea collapses, blood staining the ground beneath her. A single purple anemone drinks in the red.

She lifts her gaze. "It cannot be... Father?"

Ares says nothing at first. He watches. Measures.

Tears track down her dirt-streaked cheeks.

"Daughter," he finally says. "Why would you choose an end steeped in disgrace? So unworthy of your lineage."

"I seek only the end of this pain."

"Stand."

She forces herself upright. Every muscle screams. Her body shakes.

"I have wondered all my life what you were like. Imagining your face. If you ever knew of me."

"I know you," Ares says. "I have watched you from your first breath. Witnessed your rise with great pride. And now, you would choose death?"

She lowers her head.

"You carry my blood. To end your own life is to defy the gods... and all that we are as warriors."

Her voice, broken: "Father, I beg you. Show mercy. Take me with your own hands, as the gods did with Mother. I have nothing left."

"No."

His voice crashes like an earthquake. The forest groans.

"You will face what haunts you."

He lifts her chin. Their eyes lock.

"As a warrior must. Just as you always have."

She cannot speak. Her breath catches. Her tears fall freely.

"Now go," Ares whispers. "Be who you were born

to be."

She steps forward. Reaches for him.

Her arms wrap around him—warmth, strength, presence—

Suddenly, the sky bursts open in a thunderous explosion of light and sound. A column of flame roars upward, and Ares is torn from her grasp, lifted by divine force. The trees buckle beneath the shockwave.

Penthesilea is thrown backward, her body hitting the ground like a broken wing.

Silence.

Only the rustle of wind.

She lies there, dazed. Breathing.

She touches her stomach. Smooth skin. No wound.

Her fingers trace her throat. No blood.

Beside her, the purple anemone sways.

She exhales.

CHAPTER 30

The sea churns beneath a sky streaked with smoke and searing light. A thousand Greek ships choke the horizon, their black sails snapping like the wings of dark crows, a storm gathered for vengeance. Oars dip and rise in unison, war drums pounding from the decks, a steady, ominous rhythm echoing across the waves and into the hearts of men.

On the sands of Troy, the shore is red with ruin. War erupts like a great, living beast. Shields crash. Spears shatter. Swords sing through flesh and bone. Greek and Trojan warriors collide in a frenzy of blood and bronze, the clash of empires played out in screams and steel. The sand swallows bodies, churned into mud by the stampede of war.

From this cyclone of death, he emerges.

Achilles.

His armor is splashed crimson, the polished bronze now streaked with gore. He moves like a fury born from flame, unbound, relentless. His blade arcs through the air, a silver streak of death, and where it lands, men fall — split open like ripe fruit, their war cries silenced mid-breath.

He doesn't pause to honor them. His eyes are fixed elsewhere.

Achilles halts atop a rise in the sand, breath steady,

nostrils flared, searching. Around him, bodies writhe and fall. But his gaze drifts past it all — to one figure standing amid the chaos like a solitary pillar against the tide.

Hector.

Surrounded by the mangled forms of fallen Greeks, the Trojan prince turns.

Their eyes meet across the battlefield. And in that instant, time slows.

Hector's breath hitches in his throat. His limbs go still. He sees not just a man, but an omen. The figure that approaches him seems born from myth — a god of rage cloaked in star-speckled bronze, glinting as if the heavens themselves had forged his armor in sorrow and fury. Each step he takes thunders with certainty, with fate.

Achilles draws closer, expression etched in fire. He lifts his hands and removes his helmet.

And there they are — the eyes.

Eyes that blaze not with madness, but a vengeance so pure it burns.

"Hector. Your face is pale. Have you gazed upon your own doom?"

The words carve through the noise of war like a prophecy.

"Achilles? It cannot be. I saw you fall."

Hector's voice is strained, disbelieving — as if by naming the dead, he can keep them buried.
But the man before him stands tall, a monument to wrath and mourning.

"You saw a man I loved... wearing my armor.

Carrying my name. But now, the one you feared stands before you."

No sound follows, save the whisper of wind through broken spears. Achilles lowers the helmet over his face once more, and in that small motion, the tide of the world seems to shift.

Hector's armor is still unmarred, his limbs steady, but something within him falters. A flicker, barely visible — yet unmistakable.

For the first time, fear touches Hector's eyes.

CHAPTER 31

Dusk settles over Thermodon like a final breath. The sun bleeds gold through the tangled canopy above, its light dripping in slow rivulets over vine-strangled ruins and cracked stone pathways. Everything here is ancient, quiet, half-swallowed by the earth. The air hums with the low chant of cicadas, thick with the scent of crushed thyme and warm dust.

Through the shadowed edge of the forest, Penthesilea bursts into view.

She rides her warhorse hard, her posture upright though the journey has hollowed her. Her eyes are dark hollows rimmed in sweat and weariness, but her presence is unmistakable—she is not defeated. She is transformed. Gaunt, yes. Weathered. But reborn.

In the heart of the garden, near a dry fountain overgrown with olive branches, Melanippe stands alongside Paleos and a handful of Trojan guards. Their postures are tense, eyes wary. Something solemn lingers in the silence.

From the distance, her voice rings out, quiet but firm.

"I am sorry, but we cannot help you."

Penthesilea draws nearer, her horse slowing. Hoofbeats crunch against the gravel and fallen leaves. Melanippe turns—and sees her sister.

Her composure shatters.

A breath escapes her lips like a broken note. Her shoulders sag as if the weight of hope has suddenly returned. Without hesitation, she runs forward.

Penthesilea slides from the saddle—barely landing on her feet—before Melanippe reaches her and throws her arms around her. They cling to each other fiercely, as though even air between them would be too much distance.

"Sister. I thought you were gone forever."

"What is this?"

Penthesilea's voice is hoarse with fatigue, not yet ready for answers. She glances toward Paleos, who says nothing, though something unspoken lingers in his eyes. A heavy look passes between him and Melanippe. It says more than either dares voice aloud.

Night falls.

Inside Penthesilea's sleeping quarters, firelight flickers over stone walls and unrolled maps. Shadows stretch and quiver like silent witnesses.

Penthesilea moves with purpose. Her hands are swift, decisive, gathering salves, bread, cloth, a blade. She shoves them into a worn satchel with practiced urgency. Her jaw is clenched. Her breath steady.

In the doorway, Melanippe and Thyra watch in silence.

"You cannot do this."

"I am Queen now. Who will stop me?"

Melanippe turns, her voice cracking.

"Thyra. Say something."

"I know your sister well. Her will is iron. No words will bend it."

Thyra's voice is soft, but resolute. It lands with a weight Melanippe cannot deny. Silence fills the room—a silence of understanding, not surrender.

Melanippe steps forward, slowly. Her fingers reach for Penthesilea's free hand, curling around it.

"Please. Do not do this.

"Do not leave me alone."

Penthesilea stops. The words find her like a stone to the chest. Her eyes soften—but the steel beneath does not melt.

"What would you have me do? Hector was a friend. I cannot let his death go unanswered."

"Would Hector have done the same for you?"

The question lands hard. Not cruel, but honest. It echoes in the quiet like a challenge from the gods themselves.

Penthesilea stills. Her grip loosens. Without a word, she withdraws her hand and slings the satchel over her shoulder.

"Do you fight for him, or for the unrest within you?"

Penthesilea closes her eyes. A flicker of something cracks through her mask—grief, shame, something unnameable. When she opens them again, the glint is still there, but dimmed.

"We cared for you. And yet you vanished for days

without a word.

"And now you return, only to leave again... For a war that is not ours. For a man you barely knew."

The room holds its breath. Even the fire seems to still.

Penthesilea steps closer. Her armor shifts softly. Her eyes shimmer.

"Forgive me, sister."

She embraces Melanippe again—firmer now, more lasting. It is the kind of embrace that carries more than words.

"But I must go."

She pulls away, turns toward the door—then stops. Slowly, she returns and studies Melanippe's face, her gaze lingering.

"Antiope was wrong."

She places a hand gently over Melanippe's heart.

"You are indeed a warrior. As I have always known.

"It is time you believed it."

Tears rise to Melanippe's eyes. She swallows, but they do not fall.

Penthesilea turns to Thyra. Their eyes meet. They do not speak—not at first. There is too much in the look between them. Too much history, too much farewell.

She takes Thyra's hand. Her touch is warm. Steady.

Thyra brushes a tear from Penthesilea's cheek with the back of her hand. Her smile is gentle and full of sorrow.

Their hands part, but they do not look away.

Penthesilea opens her mouth to speak, but Thyra lifts her hand and presses two fingers to her lips. Her own tears spill freely now.

"You swore once before you would return. I dare not believe otherwise."

Penthesilea wipes Thyra's tears with the edge of her thumb. A faint smile pulls at her lips. Fragile, but real.

She leans in, and they kiss—a soft, lingering kiss. No desperation. No fear. Only reverence.

Their hands remain joined one final moment.

Then, with quiet reluctance, Penthesilea lets go.

She turns, and walks into the dark.

CHAPTER 32

The full moon hangs high over Troy, casting a pale and merciless light across the fractured city. Once-proud towers now lean like drunks, hollow and scorched. Fires flicker through shattered windows, their light stammering against walls blackened by ash. The air smells of charred wood, of burning oil, of death and waiting.

The great walls of Troy—walls built by gods—crumble like clay.

King Priam's quarters are draped in shadow, lit only by the dying embers of a brazier. The scent of incense hangs thick in the air, but it does not cleanse the weight inside the room.

Priam stands at the window, shoulders bowed beneath his robe, silhouetted by moonlight.

"Why will they not join us?"

Behind him, Paris paces, restless. Paleos stands still, hands clasped, his posture stiff with helplessness.

"The daughter of Otrera gave no reason."

Paleos's voice is low. Measured. But the words seem to thud against the stone floor like dropped armor.

Priam rubs his temples, fingers pressing against the hollowed grooves worn deep by grief. He begins to move —slow, dragging steps across the chamber, as though the air itself resists him.

"No allies. No leader. No hope. The gods have

turned their backs on Troy."

He stops. Turns to face them, eyes rimmed in shadows, voice carrying the tremble of a man watching the bones of his legacy splinter beneath him.

"Is there not anyone who can lead what is left of our army?"

"I am afraid not, my lord."

Paleos lowers his gaze, the truth bitter in his throat.

Silence descends. It is not just quiet—it is absence. The absence of answers. The absence of heroes. The slow bleeding of belief.

Then—

"That is not true."

The voice slices through the gloom. Heads snap toward the sound.

In the doorway stands Penthesilea.

A royal guardsman flanks her, but it is she who commands the space. Her presence cuts through the shadows like a drawn blade. Her armor is worn but whole. Her eyes do not waver.

Paris and Paleos glance at each other, stunned. Priam straightens, the breath caught in his chest. The guardsman steps aside without a word, as though moved by something deeper than protocol.

Penthesilea steps forward, deliberate, grounded.

"My condolences to you both. I know Hector was a great man."

"Thank you."

Priam's voice is rough, but steady.

"Forgive our shock. We were told you would not come."

"It is only I and a few others."

Paris speaks quickly, the weight in his voice lifting slightly.

"A few is better than none at all."

Priam nods slowly, then turns to Paleos with a flicker of his old authority.

"Paleos. See to it that our guests are given rooms. A restful night before battle is the least we can offer."

Paleos bows and exits, silent as ever.

"Thank you."

Penthesilea inclines her head.

"No. I am the grateful one. I owe you and your land more than words can say."

CHAPTER 33

Morning breaks over the killing fields.

A strange quiet lingers just beyond the walls of Troy, where the earth is slick with yesterday's blood. It is not peace that settles here—it is the hush before a scream. The kind of silence the gods observe when they hold their breath.

Penthesilea sits astride her mare at the crest of a shallow hill, the first light of dawn glinting off the bare bronze of her breastplate. Her helm rests in her lap, its surface dented, kissed by fire and battle. Around her, half a dozen Amazons form a loose crescent—warriors forged in sky and fire, faces solemn, limbs still. Their eyes sweep the battlefield below, where corpses lie twisted in the mud, weapons half-buried in the trampled earth. Smoke rises in thin, drifting columns.

In the distance, the sound of war continues like a rolling tide—the clamor of iron on iron, the cries of men locked in blood-pact struggle. But here, just for a breath, the world pauses.

Penthesilea inhales deeply. Her chest expands beneath the sun-scarred armor. She holds the breath for a long moment, savoring it. Then releases it.

"What a beautiful day for battle."

She exhales.

"Shall we?"

No one answers with words. They do not need to. Fingers move. Hair is pulled back and bound tightly. One by one, helmets are raised and lowered into place. Their eyes vanish behind visors of polished bronze and carved ivory. Then—

They charge.

Their war cries erupt like thunder. The horses surge forward, hooves pounding the earth in unison. The wind whips through their ranks, tearing at banners, kicking dust into the sky. They ride into the maelstrom, where the morning sun gleams off sword and shield, and the ground becomes red again.

The first Greek soldier breaks from the chaos and rushes toward them. His sword arcs upward, a flash of death in motion.

It finds her horse.

The beast lets out a strangled shriek—raw, primal —and crashes to the ground, its knees folding with a sickening crunch. Penthesilea is thrown forward. The air leaves her lungs as she hits the dirt, but she lands hard on her feet, crouched, blade ready.

No time to think.

Another swing from the same soldier—a downward cut meant to split her skull. She lifts her sword and meets the blow with a deafening clash. The shock ripples through her arms. She pivots, knees flexed, and with a savage upward stroke, opens his belly in a splash of red.

Their eyes meet. There is something in his gaze—a

flicker of recognition, then fear.

She kicks him backward, hard. He falls, writhing, and the blood seeps into the thirsty earth.

A scream cuts through the haze—a new enemy surges toward her, sword raised high. Their blades collide with a furious clamor. He is strong. His momentum drives her back. Her heel strikes something—a jagged rock buried in the mud—and she falls, hard onto her back.

The Greek lunges. His boot crashes down on her wrist, pinning her sword to the dirt. She grits her teeth as pain flashes up her arm. His blade rises, gleaming.

But her other hand finds the haft of her axe.

She swings it low.

The blade cleaves into the soft joint of his knee. His scream splits the air, sharp and jagged. He buckles. She rips the axe free and, with a fluid motion born of rage and necessity, brings it down again—this time across his neck.

His head separates cleanly. His body slumps onto her, hot blood soaking into her chestplate. The copper tang floods her nose.

She shoves the corpse aside, breath ragged. Her face is smeared with crimson now—not just theirs, but hers. Her muscles tremble. Her eyes do not blink.

She rises.

Ahead of her, three more Greeks step into view. Their armor gleams, unmarred. Fresh warriors. Fresh steel. They fan out around her, blades at the ready, eyes scanning her stance.

Penthesilea exhales slowly.

She rolls her shoulders. Adjusts her grip. The blood on her palms makes the hilt slick, but she does not falter. She nods once, and steps forward.

CHAPTER 34

War is no longer a moment—it is a tide.

It roars across the plains outside Troy, swallowing all in its path.

Penthesilea moves like a storm-goddess incarnate. Her arms are slick with blood—some of it hers, most of it not. She cuts down the first soldier with a swift slash across the throat; the wound opens in a wet gasp, and he collapses, grasping at nothing. The second she meets chest to chest—her axe driving deep, the haft trembling in her grip as bone splinters. The third lunges. She twists behind him, seizes his chin with one hand, the crown of his head with the other, and *snaps*. His body spasms once, then folds to the ground like a broken puppet.

All around her, the Amazons descend like the wrath of Artemis.

They ride through the Greek lines with the fury of thunderclouds. Hooves tear up the earth, blades flash in arcs of molten silver. Limbs fly. Men scream. Shields are split like ripe fruit. Their war cries are sharp, wild, echoing across the field like the call of hunting hawks. Dust and blood rise in spirals beneath them.

Paris fights with a quiet desperation. He is not loud, not glorious. He is surgical. His sword strikes fast and vanishes. A Greek soldier lifts his blade—Paris ducks, pivots, and drives steel into his ribs before the breath leaves the man's chest. He does not wait to watch him fall. Another comes. Another dies. He moves like fire through dry grass, consuming without hesitation.

Penthesilea finds herself surrounded again.

Five Greeks this time—bigger, broader, emboldened by numbers. They circle her, feet crunching over armor and corpses. Their breath fogs in the morning air. Their blades glint.

They lunge.

Not together. Not cleanly. One jerks forward with a scream, and the others follow in scattered rhythm. Metal glints in the rising sun. Blades slash downward, sideward, thrust at her belly, her chest, her throat.

She moves.

She spins low, ducking one strike, her foot snapping a shinbone with a brutal kick. Another swings wide—she drops her axe and catches his wrist mid-arc, twisting until it breaks with a sickening crack. Her sword sings as it rises—opening a throat, splitting a jaw, sliding through ribs. The last of them stumbles back, wounded but stubborn. She leaps—driving her knee into his chest, her blade punching through his eye. He collapses without a sound.

Steel clatters to the ground. Blood pools in jagged shadows.

The sun sets.

It does not fall gently.

It bleeds out across the ruined plain, a final golden hemorrhage painting broken helmets and the lifeless faces beneath them. Spears lie like bones cracked in half. Horses twitch in their last breaths. Arrows stick upright from the earth like grave markers. All around: silence. Not absence, but aftermath.

Penthesilea stands alone in that stillness, her body streaked in red, arms slack at her sides, sword dragging slightly behind her in the dust.

She lifts her eyes skyward.

The sky is bruised purple and red, and in its deepest place—where the light has truly died—Sirius gleams. Cold. Bright. Unflinching. The dog star.

She stares up as though listening.

A warrior's omen. The gods have seen her.

Morning.

The new day arrives without ceremony.

There is no trumpet. No song. Only the stirring of dust as the wind curls along the bones of the battlefield. The sky glows amber, tinged with smoke and blood. It is soft — deceptively gentle — like silk drawn across a sword's edge.

Then—

Footsteps.

Not many. Just one pair.

Slow. Measured. Terrible.

Each step lands like a funeral drum, steady and resonant. Sand shifts beneath armored boots. Loose stones crack. The clink of bronze greaves. The low hum of purpose in motion.

Achilles.

He emerges from the haze like a revenant. Not a man. Not a warrior. Something older. Something holy. His sword rests in one hand, relaxed. Ready. There is no rush in him — only inevitability.

He advances.

And where he walks, men die.

A Trojan leaps from behind a wrecked chariot — Achilles doesn't even turn. His sword whips around in a tight, brutal arc. The Trojan's head lifts into the air, trailing red, and hits the ground with a wet thud. Another charges — he's skewered mid-sprint, his momentum sliding him down Achilles' blade like meat on a spit.

He moves forward, expression unchanged.

He is not fighting.

He is executing.

Penthesilea returns to the fray like a storm breaking free of the sea.

She does not wait. She does not think. She *becomes*. Her blade spins from her hand, slashing the knee of one soldier before she catches it again. Her axe crashes through a shield, snapping the wrist behind it. She punches the man with her elbow as he screams, and when he falls, she follows with a downward cut that splits him from clavicle to hip.

Each swing is precise. Sacred. A war hymn in motion.

Paris moves like a blade himself.

He does not roar. He does not look for glory. He fights to *survive*. His feet never stop moving. He slips between two Greeks, parries a thrust, and cuts low — severing tendons. A spear comes from the right — he ducks and throws a knife into the soldier's throat before rising again with his sword.

He is not a prince now.

He is necessity. Speed. Cunning. Fire wrapped in skin.

Swords clash.

Not like in stories — no clean ringing chime. They slam together in violence. In desperation. Sparks fly. Edges scrape and grind. Every clash is a promise: *I will not die today.*

Spears arc.

They sail through the sky like ancient omens, the sun flashing off their tips. They fall not in lines but in chaos, burying themselves in sand, shield, bone. Each one a silent scream from above.

Flesh splits.

Skin parts like silk torn too fast. Blood fans into the air, painting the dead and the living alike. Men drop to their knees, hands pressed to wounds they don't have time to understand. Eyes stare into nothing.

The battlefield does not choose. It devours.

Friend. Foe. Young. Old. Hero. Coward. It eats them all the same.

Dusk.

There is no count that can capture it.

Just rows of bodies. Stacked. Tangled. Smeared. The groaning of the half-dead beneath tents of torn cloth. Priests murmur prayers over those who will not see the next sun. Swords are sharpened by hands that cannot stop shaking.

A New Day.

The sun returns.

But it is not a sunrise.

It is a burning eye, indifferent to the piles of corpses below.

The war continues.

Achilles mounts his horse, blade sheathed, armor gleaming like a god's mirror. He kicks once. The beast surges forward. Greek ranks part before him. He does not slow. Every swing lands. Every strike ends. The ground drinks again.

Penthesilea charges through the ranks like a river that cannot be dammed. Her sword arcs. Her axe splits helmets. She roars. Not from rage—but because it is the only sound left inside her.

Paris is still moving. Still striking. Still breathing.

Days pass.

The sun rises. The sun falls. Over and over. And with it, more blood.

The ground becomes too thick to bury. Too loud to mourn. Glory has weight now. And it stinks of rot.

From thousands, only hundreds remain.

Penthesilea stands above a trembling Greek soldier, her blade resting at his throat.

She says nothing.

Her eyes tell him everything.

She gestures. *Run.*

He does.

But mercy is always a risk.

A flash of bronze.

A kopis blade tears into her side, slicing deep beneath her ribs. The pain sears. She stumbles, teeth clenched. The world tilts.

She roars.

Her sword rises like vengeance itself and crashes down, splitting helm and skull in one final stroke. The man's body drops, twitching.

She grabs the knife in her side and rips it free with a snarl.

Blood pours. She does not cry out.

She limps forward, every step a prayer, every

breath a refusal to fall.
        The sun dips again behind her.
        She does not look back.

Chapter 35

Mourning Light

The sun hangs low but harsh above the war camp, casting long shadows across a field lined with sagging tents and shattered spears. Flies hum over bloodied bandages. The stench of death, sweat, and sour wine lingers in the morning air like smoke that won't rise.

Penthesilea steps from her tent, fully armed.

Her armor—streaked, cracked—catches the pale gold of dawn. Across her back rests a quiver of obsidian-tipped arrows. At her hip, the worn hilt of her sword shifts with each stride. Her face is unreadable—chiseled from focus and fatigue. This morning is like all the ones before it: quiet, bitter, and soaked in the silence between battles.

Paris strides past.

His tunic is torn, the linen dark with dried blood. His lip is split, and one eye bears the purple bloom of a hard-earned bruise. He walks with the stiffness of someone who hasn't slept in days, but when he sees her, he slows.

Penthesilea doesn't look his way.

"Paris. Good to see you are still with us."

Her tone is dry, almost indifferent—like they were passing in a palace corridor rather than a blood-soaked encampment.

Paris halts. Turns toward her. She remains facing forward, shoulders squared.

"I desire to offer an apology."

She glances over her shoulder. An arched brow.

"For what cause, precisely?"

"I misspoke. My words at dinner were poorly chosen."

He hesitates, then adds:

"Having witnessed the full measure of your capabilities… I thought it right to acknowledge it."

"It is not necessary."

A pause stretches between them. The wind tugs gently at the tent flaps, the only movement in an otherwise frozen camp.

Paris exhales, a scoff under his breath—not bitter, just tired.

"The Greeks keep coming. Each day, more blood."

"It shows no sign of ending."

"I grow weary. So many great Trojan warriors just… gone."

His voice tightens. His jaw shifts. He forces the name forward.

"Hector."

He swallows hard.

"I shoulder the burden of defending my home alone."

She steps forward—not quickly, but with purpose. Her shadow stretches toward his in the dirt.

"You are not alone."

There is no softness in her voice, but there is weight. The kind of truth only warriors offer—not comfort, but kinship.

For a long moment, neither moves.

Then Paris nods and begins to turn.

"Paris."

He pauses. Looks back.

"You, too, hold your own with a blade. Troy is fortunate to have you. Hector would nod with pride."

Something shifts behind his eyes. Grief is there, yes—but so is something quieter. Something warmer. Less burdened.

"As would Hippolyta."

A faint smile touches his lips. Small. True.

Without another word, he moves on.

Across the field, the Greek camp is a shadow of its former self.

Once proud and orderly, it now lies strewn with the detritus of attrition. Torn banners sag above slumping tents. Armor lies scattered—some unclaimed, some unwearable. The wounded groan beneath makeshift coverings, too many to count. The scent of rot clings to the dew-soaked air.

Achilles sits on a large boulder just beyond his tent.

He tears at a hunk of barley bread with the same intensity he once reserved for battle. A shallow bowl of figs rests beside him—untouched, their skins puckered and dull. His gaze sweeps the camp—not searching, just taking silent inventory of what remains.

He sees the broken men. The missing faces. The

quiet.

He rises.

His body is still that of a demigod—untouched by age or exhaustion, carved by vengeance—but his eyes betray it. They burn not with fire, but with a weariness too deep to name.

"Can any among you say why our men fall in such number?"

His voice cracks the silence like a thunderclap. Heads turn—but no one speaks.

Only silence.

With a growl, he hurls the bread aside. It lands in the dust with a dull thud. The bowl of figs goes flying, kicked from his path. They burst open on the ground, their pulp seeping into the soil.

A soldier steps forward—slowly, carefully. His armor is mismatched. His eyes downcast.

It is the same soldier Penthesilea once spared.

"Sir."

Achilles turns. His gaze is fire—hot, unblinking, patient in its danger.

"I come bearing a message."

"From?"

"A Trojan… seeking the man who took the life of Prince Hector."

Achilles' breath hitches—almost imperceptibly.

His nostrils flare. His jaw tightens, stone beneath skin.

The camp holds its breath.

The figs stain the earth at his feet. The wind refuses to move.

And Achilles says nothing.

Not yet.

CHAPTER 36

Grey light stretches across the battlefield's heart like a veil of ash. The sun, low and smothered, casts no warmth. Dust coils in lazy spirals, carried on a wind too tired to howl. Horses snort in the distance, tossing their heads to shake free the grit from their nostrils.

All has gone still.

Greek and Trojan alike form a loose ring around the center of the field. No swords clash. No arrows fly. For this moment, the war waits. The earth seems to hold its breath.

At the center, Achilles stands—his bronze helm crested with horsehair, eyes narrow beneath the shadow of fate. His stance is steady, his breath calm. His sword hangs at his side, loose in his grip.

Opposite him: Penthesilea. Her face shielded by her crusted helmet—only revealing her eyes and the bend in her lips.

Her blade is dark with blood. Her armor, battered and scorched. Still, she stands tall—despite the limp in her step, the tremble in her limbs. The sand beneath her feet is stained, but she is untouched by fear. Gravity does not hold her—the fire in her veins does.

A single breath passes.

Then—they charge.

Their swords collide with a thunderclap that rolls

across the field like sky cracking open. Steel meets steel with raw fury. Sparks leap as their blades crash again and again. Penthesilea sidesteps—fluid, fast—her feet gliding over the sand like wind-dancers.

Achilles steadies his blade with a pinch of his fingers, shifting his stance to absorb her speed.

"You fight fiercely and speak not."

She offers no answer. Only her eyes respond—sharp, unyielding, unreadable.

"Is that silence pride... or fear?"

They circle.

Slow. Poised. Coiled like predators. Neither blinking. Neither yielding. Each step deliberate. Each breath measured.

Then Achilles strikes.

He crashes into her like a wave against rock. Their swords flash, then clash. His shield slams into her chest with brutal force. She stumbles, coughing—but she does not fall. Instead, she surges forward, blade slicing low.

Steel shrieks. Sparks fly.

A storm of blows follows—blades ringing, clashing, echoing. He feints. She counters. He lunges. She pivots.

Her sword cuts across his bicep. Blood sprays in a vivid arc.

Gasps ripple through the onlookers.

Achilles glances at the wound, then at her. Their eyes lock.

"You do not move like one born of Troy."

He charges again.

His shield hammers into her with even greater force. She crashes to the ground. Sand explodes around her. Achilles looms above—sword raised, eyes hard.

"I have heard of your wrath. They say you have claimed a hundred of my men. A warrior without fear. Without mercy."

He pauses.

"And yet before me, I see a man who defies those tales."

She rolls free, kicks up dust, rises with a snarl—and hurls herself at him.

Steel crashes. Sparks leap.

She ducks low—fast and sudden.

He twists, but not fast enough. Her blade slashes the back of his calf. Blood pours. She falters. He lunges.

The sand drinks their pain.

Still, she rises.

Sword in hand. Unbowed.

She lifts her chin and beckons with a flick of her fingers.

Come.

He answers.

They collide in a whirlwind of fury. He strikes high. She rolls beneath his blade, slashing upward. Her sword slices deep across his back.

Achilles grunts—falls to one knee.

Blood stains his tunic.

Teeth gritted, he forces himself up.

"Have we not danced long enough? Time to end it."

He brings his shield forward. She pounds her blade against it. Once. Twice. Again. He holds steady. Then his sword slips low—cutting her shin.

She growls. Her blade answers—slashing his ribs. A thin line of red blooms along his side.

With a roar, Achilles casts his shield aside. It crashes behind him.

They clash again—faster, harder, breathless. Her elbow slams his jaw. His head snaps back. He drops. Helmet skids across the dust.

Before he rises, she lunges. Her arm wraps around his throat in a brutal hold.

He chokes, clawing.

Desperate, he drives his sword downward— through her foot, into the ground.

Penthesilea screams.

Her grip shatters. Blood spills from the wound.

Panting, she braces against her sword, dragging herself upright on one leg. She sways—but she stands.

Achilles watches.

"You are a true warrior," he says quietly.

His lips twitch. His eyes still blaze.

"Brave... or reckless. Perhaps both."

With a roar, he charges.

She meets him.

Swords collide again. Their breath mingles. Their faces are inches apart. They grunt. They snarl. Steel grinds against steel.

She drives her knee into his groin.

Achilles collapses sideways, a groan torn from his chest.

She limps toward him, eyes glare in grim defiance.

He rises—sword in hand.

They strike. Again. And again. Relentless. Violent. Each blow closer, louder, sharper.

Then—at the same moment—they reach for their daggers.

Penthesilea is faster.

Her blade drives into his side.

He gasps. Eyes wide. They're face to face. Bloodied. Breathless.

Something fierce lives in the space between them— intimate. Terrible. Not hate. Not yet love.

Just knowing.

Then—

The whisper of steel through flesh.

Penthesilea gasps.

Her dagger slips from her hand.

Blood wells at her lips.

Achilles stares into her eyes.

The wound is mortal. They both know it.

She stumbles. Falls. Her body folds into the earth like something sacred returning to dust.

A dagger juts from her chest. The hilt trembles.

The sun kisses the horizon. Stars blink into the violet sky.

Her gaze drifts upward. Her lips part.

"Mother?"

From the dusk, a vision forms.

Otrera. Radiant. Smiling.

Peace settles on Penthesilea's face.

Her fingers stretch skyward. Her breath slows.

Slows…

Then stops.

Her sword slips from her hand. It lands in the sand with a soft, final thud.

Achilles kneels beside her.

Gently, reverently, he removes her helmet.

Her hair spills out—dark as wine, streaked with blood and firelight. Her face is still, but aglow—flushed with something divine.

She is not merely beautiful.

She is otherworldly.

Achilles gazes down at her.

His jaw slackens. His chest rises—once, twice—with a quiet ache.

He brushes a lock of hair from her brow. Touches the corner of her mouth.

"No warrior has ever met my blade with such fire."

His voice breaks.

He does not look like a conqueror.

He looks like a man undone.

Not with desire.

But with reverence.

The battlefield is silent.

No soldier moves.

The circle remains—Greeks and Trojans still as

statues.

Achilles lifts her in his arms.

He holds her the way he once held Patroclus.

Gently. Brokenly.

He walks.

Menelaus steps forward, uncertain.

"Achilles. Where are you taking her?"

Achilles does not speak.

Dust stirs at his feet.

The soldiers part—without command. Like waves for a passing god.

Chapter 37

Ash and Anemone

The sun has fled.

In its absence, the moon reigns—cold and sovereign, casting silver light over the black, whispering sea. Waves lap against the shore in tireless hushes, like the world itself mourns, breath held in reverence.

Achilles walks into the surf.

His armor is gone. His weapons are sheathed, discarded, or forgotten. His hands are bare, cradling her broken form against his chest with a reverence that defies war. He moves slowly, deliberately—each step pressing into the soaked sand, each one surrendered to the tide as it pulls at his heels like a spirit reluctant to let him pass.

The sea rises around his thighs, churning with salt and silence.

It touches her limbs. It touches her wounds.

Salt meets blood.

And it is no longer the aftermath of battle—it is ritual.

Not cleansing, but consecration.

He kneels.

Submerging her gently beneath the dark water, he holds her as though the sea might carry her soul beyond reach of the gods. Her hair fans out beneath the surface like midnight threads, floating free. Her skin, once fire-warm with fury and will, lies pale under the moon. The tide washes the blood from her brow, from her fingers, from the silent wound at her side—touching her with the tenderness of a mother tending a child.

Achilles does not weep.

He only breathes—shallow, broken, trembling against the night.

Then, he lifts her again.

Water streams from her limbs, glistening like memory. She does not resist. She is weight. She is silence. She is all that remains. He rises with her in his arms and walks slowly back toward the beach, toward the flicker of torchlight that waits in hushes between the wind.

The waves recede behind him like an oath unspoken.

Night deepens.

On the shore, a pyre has been built—not from haste, but from intention.

Each log placed with reverence. Each stone laid like a tribute.

A warrior's farewell.

Penthesilea lies at its center—not swathed in linen, but in white anemones. Hundreds. Thousands. Their petals luminous in the moonlight, draped across her body like snow that refuses to melt. They are sacred to the Amazons. Sacred to Otrera. A symbol of battle and beauty. Of life that demands to be remembered.

Achilles stands before her.

A single torch burns in his hand, its flame small and alive.

His face is a map of grief—lines deepened not by war, but by something heavier. His eyes are hollowed by what cannot be undone. He stares at her and sees not conquest, not glory, but the undoing of everything that once made him certain.

He does not blink.

"They will sing of my victory," he says quietly.

The torch trembles. His knuckles whiten around it.

"But your death will haunt me."

He lowers the flame.

It kisses the base of the pyre like a secret shared with the earth.

The fire breathes—soft at first. A hush. Then a hiss. Then a roar.

The anemones curl. Their petals blacken. The fire consumes gently, then hungrily—climbing, devouring. The wood snaps beneath the rising heat, embers dancing skyward like sparks of memory. The flames gild her body in golden light—one final warmth before surrender.

Penthesilea does not move.

But she is not hollow.

Her face is serene, sculpted in stillness. No agony. No fear.

Only rest. Only release.

She burns not as a casualty of war—but as a tribute to the gods.

An offering worthy of Olympus.

Ash begins to rise.

Light as breath. Glowing like forgotten stars. It spirals upward into the sky, drawn toward the heavens. The smoke mingles with the night, and above them all, Sirius burns—bright and unyielding. The Dog Star. The eternal sentinel. Watching.

Achilles does not move.

Not as the last flame dies to cinder.

Not as the wind scatters the ashes.

Not as the tide creeps forward again, drawn to what was taken.

He remains, long after the others have gone.

Still as the stones. Quiet as the stars.

Staring into the darkness that remains.

And in his chest, something sharp and quiet lodges deep.

A name. A face. A moment.

Not conquered.

But remembered.

EPILOGUE

What Follows the Flame...

They say Paris, prince of Troy, did not scream when he loosed the arrow.

He stood atop the ramparts—arms steady, gaze unwavering—guided by fate... or perhaps by Apollo's own hand. The shaft sang as it flew, a sliver of vengeance loosed into the heavens. It struck Achilles in the one place no bronze or blade had ever pierced: his heel.

The mighty warrior staggered.

The gods held their breath.

And the man who could not be stopped—who had danced with death, who had brought queens and kings and demigods to their knees—fell.

He did not die with a cry, but in silence, as if slipping back into the underworld he had never truly left.

The Greeks, bloodied and desperate, feigned retreat.

They left behind a gift—a monument taller than the gates of Troy. A horse of impossible scale, carved from wood and etched with the marks of surrender.

The Trojans, wearied by war and blinded by hope, welcomed it into their city. The massive beast rolled over the shattered threshold, hailed as an offering to Athena.

But when night cloaked the city, and Troy exhaled in triumph—

The Greeks emerged from its hollow belly.

Fire erupted in the streets.

Blades flashed through palaces.

Families were dragged from sleep into slaughter.

By dawn, the city once kissed by gods—blessed, defiant, radiant—was reduced to ash.

Troy did not fall with peace, but with the silence of stone.

Helen returned to Sparta.

Menelaus, king once more, took her hand and led her across the dark sea. For days, no words passed between them—only the groan of timbers, the snap of sails, and the quiet mourning of gulls.

In Sparta, they lived out their days in uneasy peace.

She was loved again, though not as before.

And he ruled again, though never with pride.

They rarely spoke of Troy.

But sometimes, in the flicker of firelight, Helen would lift her gaze to the stars—searching. Remembering.

Years passed.

The Amazons did not forget.

A small band of warriors, cloaked in black and dust, rode east beneath moonless skies. They did not seek the ashes of Achilles to steal—but to avenge. To face the one who had taken their queen. Through wind and storm,

over rivers and wastelands, they rode until they reached
his tomb by the sea.

There, they found his ghost.

He rose from the mist like a revenant, tall and
silent, rimmed in frost.

The horses screamed.

They reared and spun, eyes wide with terror, foam
at their mouths.

Warriors were thrown like leaves in a tempest.
They scrambled to their feet, breath ragged, pride broken.

None dared draw steel.

They fled.

Their retreat was quiet—but bitter. No songs were
sung that night.

But time, too, kneels.

And memory becomes myth.

Penthesilea, queen of the Amazons, is no longer
flesh and blood—but legend. Her name etched into bronze.
Her story carried on the wind through the mountain
passes. They say no warrior—neither god, nor king, nor
destiny itself—could match her.

She is not remembered for how she died.

But for how she lived.

Sword in hand.

Head high.

Bloodied and unbroken.

Staring down gods, unafraid.

Penthesilea.

The greatest of all Amazons.

And the last warrior Achilles ever loved.

About the Author

Stephanie Vanise is a film and television editor turned writer. Her editing credits include critically acclaimed series such as *Atypical* and the Peabody Award-winning *Surviving R. Kelly.*

When industry shifts led to fewer opportunities in post-production, she turned to writing as a way to continue exploring meaningful, creative storytelling.

Stephanie lives in Los Angeles, California, with her beloved dog, Zayla.

To learn more, visit www.stephanieneroes.com

www.ingramcontent.com/pod-product-compliance
Lightning Source LLC
Chambersburg PA
CBHW032250310726
48973CB00008B/2365